HEALING HEARTS LARGE PRINT

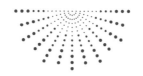

RUTH HARTZLER

ROMANCE BOOKS

GLOSSARY

Pennsylvania Dutch is a dialect, not a language, because it has no standard written form. It is written as it sounds, which is why you will see the same word written several different ways. All are permissible.

The word 'Dutch' has nothing to do with Holland, but rather is likely a corruption of the German word 'Deitsch' or 'Deutsch'.

ab im kopp - addled in the head

Ach! (also, Ack!) - Oh!

aenti - aunt

appeditlich - delicious

Ausbund - Amish hymn book

bedauerlich - sad

bloobier - blueberry

boppli - baby

bopplin - babies

bro - bread

bruder(s) - brother(s)

bu - boy

Budget, The - weekly newspaper for Amish and Mennonite communities. Based on Sugarcreek, Ohio, and has 2 versions, Local and National.

buwe - boys

daag - day

Daed, Datt, Dat (vocative) - Dad

Diary, The - Lancaster County based Amish newspaper. Focus is on Old Order Amish.

Dawdi (also, Daadi) (vocative) - Grandfather

dawdi haus (also, daadi haus, grossdawdi haus) - grandfather's or grandparents' house (often a small house behind the main house)

de Bo - boyfriend

Die Botschaft - Amish weekly newspaper. Based in PA but its focus is nation-wide.

demut - humility

denki (or danki, denke) - thank you

Der Herr - The Lord

dochder - daughter

dokter - doctor

doplich - clumsy

dumm - dumb

dummkopf - idiot, dummy

Dutch Blitz - Amish card game

English (or Englisch) (adjective) - A non-Amish person

Englischer (noun) - A non-Amish person

familye - family

ferhoodled - foolish, crazy

fraa - wife, woman

froh - happy

freind - friend

freinden - friends

gegisch - silly

geh - go

gern gheschen (also, gern gschehne) - you're welcome

Gott (also, Gotte) - God

grank - sick, ill

grossboppli - grandbaby

grossdawdi (also, dawdi, daadi haus, gross dawdi) - grandfather, or, in some communities, great grandfather

grosskinskind - great-grandchild

grosskinskinner - great-grandchildren

grossmammi (or grossmudder) - grandmother

gross-sohn - grandson

grossvadder - grandfather (see also grossdawdi)

gude mariye - good morning

guten nacht (also, gut nacht) - good night

gude nochmiddaag - good afternoon

gut - good

haus - house

Herr - Mr.

Hiya - Hi

hochmut - pride

Hullo (also, Hallo) - Hello

hungerich - hungry

Ich liebe dich - I love you

jah (also ya) - yes

kaffi (also, kaffee) - coffee

kapp - prayer covering worn by women

kichli - cookie

kichlin - cookies

kinn (also, kind) - child

kinner - children

kinskinner - Grandchildren

Kumme (or Kumm) - Come

lieb - love, sweetheart

liewe - a term of endearment, dear, love

liede - song

maid (also, maed) - girls

maidel (also, maedel) - girl

Mamm (also, Mammi) - Mother, Mom

Mammi - Grandmother

mann - man

mariye-esse - breakfast

mei - my

meidung - shunning

mei lieb - my love

mein liewe - my dear, my love

menner - men

mudder - mother

naerfich - nervous

naut (also, nacht) - night

nee (also nein) - no

nix - nothing

nohma - name

onkel - uncle

Ordnung - "Order", the unwritten Amish set of rules, different in each community

piffle (also, piddle) - to waste time or kill time

Plain - referring to the Amish way of life

rett (also, redd) - to put (items) away or to clean up.

rootsh (also, ruch) - not being able to sit still.

rumspringa (also, rumschpringe) - Running around years - when Amish youth (usually around the age of sixteen) leave the community for time and can be English, and decide whether to commit to the Amish way of life and be baptized.

schatzi - honey

schee - pretty, handsome

schecklich - scary

schmaert - smart

schtupp - family room

schweschder - sister

schweschdern - sisters

schwoger - brother-in-law

seltsam - strange, unnatural

sohn - son

vadder - father

verboten - forbidden

Vorsinger - Song leader

was its let - what is the matter?

wie gehts - how are you?

wilkum (also, wilkom) - welcome

wunderbar (also, wunderbaar) - wonderful

yer - you

yourself - yourself

youngie (also, young) - the youth

yung - young

CHAPTER ONE

Diana stared at the rain bouncing on the restaurant windows before sighing and turning her attention back to her date. Nick was a colleague at the advertising agency firm of Sellers and Tome. Despite the fact they were both in line for the same promotion, he had been awfully nice to her of late.

Jethro's image arose before her, and she pushed it out of her mind as she always did. Sighing, Diana avoided the thoughts of what might have been. Jethro was Amish, and there was no way she could ever join the community. Sure, once she'd thought she could become Amish, but then she'd changed her mind. Jethro, no doubt, had married years ago. Diana never had.

Diana had been living in New York for the past ten years. Work as an advertising executive had consumed her, and the long hours had kept her from feeling too constricted and claustrophobic in her tiny studio apartment on Park Avenue. Diana's allowance had stopped as soon as she graduated from school, and although her job paid well, New York was expensive, far more expensive than Lancaster County.

Diana's life had been one of privilege, being raised at Hawk Mountain Manor, originally a Pennsylvania German stone farmhouse which had been substantially expanded over the years. The manor sat on over one hundred acres of lush pastures and woodland. A tiny studio flat was a far cry from what Diana had been used to, but at least it kept her far away from painful memories.

The sounds of Nick clearing his throat brought her back to the present. "What time's your presentation with the clients?"

"Ten on Thursday."

Nick nodded. "Best of luck with it. Mine's on Friday." He reached across and patted her hand. "May the best man—sorry, man or *woman*—win. Now, tell me all about your presentation."

Diana had just finished telling Nick the details of her presentation when the waiter arrived. He deposited steaming plates in front of them: for Nick, Filet Mignon with roasted garlic-parmesan fingerling potatoes, baby spinach, and horseradish pepper sauce, and for Diana, chicken sautéed in white wine with garlic, rosemary, and lemon.

The conversation lapsed, and they ate in

silence. Diana was not attracted to Nick—he seemed nice enough, but there was no spark, not like she'd had with Jethro.

She had loved their picnics. Just her and Jethro, down by the sparkling pond. She would always pack the same meal—ham and Camembert baguette sandwiches. Soggy sandwiches were the bane of Diana's existence, so she used only the lightest spread of fig jam to keep the baguette crusty. After tucking in a few slices of ham and a wedge of cheese, she'd wrap the sandwiches in paper and place them carefully in the basket, which Jethro would lift from his buggy.

She had loved walking through the sweet, warm air down to the water's edge with Jethro at her side. Had she ever packed a picnic basket for Nick? No, because he would have laughed at the simplicity of the activity.

Nick liked expensive restaurants. He liked posting about them on social media, showing off for all his friends. He would have laughed at Jethro, at Jethro's love and respect for his family. Nick didn't speak to his family. He didn't like that they were poor, and that he was raised in a home that his current friends would have laughed at.

"Shall we sit here?" Jethro had always asked, even though Diana and Jethro always sat in exactly the same spot. He was courteous like that. In fact, Diana had never again met a man as polite and softly spoken as her Jethro. But he wasn't her Jethro any more, was he? She'd made that decision, and in the process had broken both of their hearts.

"That would be lovely," Diana had replied to Jethro. "Thank you."

He really was a strapping man. His muscles were big and hard from the physical labor he did every day. That was the thing about the Amish—no one valued hard work as much as they did, and Diana respected that so much.

Working hard in a field would have straightened Nick out, but she would never say that to him. Nick was vain and egotistical, and he believed he was perfect in every way.

Jethro would not have known what to make of Nick, but he would still have treated him with decency and respect. Nick laughed at people he did not understand.

"*Denki* for the picnic," Jethro always said as he unwrapped his sandwiches.

Diana loved seeing him eat the food she had prepared, even if it was something so easy to make. He was so appreciative of her efforts that she felt her cheeks burn with delight whenever she was fortunate enough to find herself sprawling on the grass with him.

Yes, this was not the life she had ever imagined for herself. The Amish had always seemed so simple and imprisoned by that simplicity in Diana's eyes, but now she saw there was so much freedom in being Amish, in having so many choices removed. She had always felt overwhelmed by the mall with its hundreds of stores, and by the overt advertising that lined the walls. Children shopped in the mall, and children were flooded with inappropriate images every time they stepped out of their homes. But Amish children were not. Amish children got to be children, and Amish adults were not trapped by their lack of choices but empowered.

The Amish focused on what mattered, and what mattered was family and God. It was a beautiful lifestyle, one that had almost belonged to Diana.

The waiter appearing with the dessert menus brought Diana back to the present. She had only glanced briefly at the menu when Nick's phone rang. "I'm terribly sorry," he said. "I'll have to take this." He stood up and walked out of sight.

Diana looked through the dessert menu and

waited for him to return. She didn't have to wait long. Nick tapped her on the shoulder. "I'm sorry, Diana. It's an emergency. I have to leave. I'll see you at work tomorrow. Wednesday's your morning off, isn't it?"

"Yes," Diana began, but Nick had already left. Seconds later, she realized he had left her with the bill.

D iana arrived at work at precisely twelve noon the next day. As Diana walked into the offices, one of the junior assistants caught her by the arm. "Diana, I have to speak with you." She drew her close to the wall.

"What is it?" Diana asked, trickles of apprehension running up her spine.

The woman looked around before whispering, "It's about your presentation, the one you were supposed to give on Friday. Nick called the clients in early and presented to them this morning. I overheard him bragging to Barry that he presented your ideas to them."

Diana was horrified. "Are you sure? There must be some mistake."

The woman shook her head before hurrying away.

Diana stood there in shock until the receptionist called her over. "Colleen wants to see you right away."

Diana bit her lip. She didn't have a meeting scheduled with Colleen, her boss, so surely this was bad news, especially if Nick had, in fact, stolen her ideas and presented them to the clients. Or maybe this was about the promotion. She knew she would hear news of the promotion soon, but she had thought Colleen would wait until after the presentations. Maybe, Colleen had made her mind up already.

Colleen's door was open. She wasted no time waving Diana inside. "Come in, Diana. Shut the door behind you. Have a seat." She gestured to the transparent plastic chair in front of her. Diana had always figured it was some sort of designer chair. As she sat on the hard, uncomfortable chair, she searched Colleen's face for clues, but Colleen's expression was impassive.

Colleen's hair was an impossible shade of red matched by the frames of her glasses. She popped them down her nose and looked over the top of them at Diana. "It's not good news," she began. "I'll come straight to the point. Nick has the promotion, not you."

Diana gasped, despite her attempts to appear neutral. "But why?" she asked in a small voice. "I thought you were waiting until after the presentations."

"Nick gave his presentation this morning,"

Colleen said. "The clients were so impressed that they hired him on the spot."

"But, but Nick told me his presentation was on Friday morning."

Colleen raised one eyebrow. "Diana, you have good creative skills and you're well-organized, but I'm afraid you're a little naïve. This is a cutthroat business, and you lack the killer instant to succeed."

Colleen continued to talk, but Diana wasn't listening. Nick had tricked her! He had been dating her and had invited her to dinner the previous night simply to extract information from her. How could she have been so foolish? How could she think a good-looking man like Nick would be interested in someone like her? Surely, Nick could have a younger, better-looking woman.

She was silently chiding herself when her phone rang. "I'm terribly sorry, Colleen," she said. "I forgot to turn it off before our meeting."

She fumbled in her purse, but the phone had stopped ringing by the time she found it. A text message soon followed. Diana looked at it and gasped. "My father's had a heart attack!"

"Where does he live?"

"Pennsylvania."

Colleen waved one hand at her. "Then take the week off."

Diana made to protest, but Colleen continued. "I insist. Take a week or two off and decide whether this business is for you. If it is, you'll have to toughen up and stop being so gullible."

With that, Diana was dismissed from the office.

CHAPTER TWO

The drive to Hawk Mountain Manor in Pennsylvania passed by in a blur. Diana was alone with her thoughts, and they were not happy ones.

As she approached the manor, the homesickness that Diana had denied herself for ten long years threatened to overwhelm her. The drive through the woods and manicured pastures just before the entrance to the manor left Diana on the point of tears.

An Amish buggy drawn by a flashy bay horse

passed her going the other way. She was back in Amish country now—there was no denying it. Would she be able to avoid Jethro? She certainly hoped so. At any rate, she hadn't been home in years and she doubted he would recognize her. She was ten years older and, much to her regret, several pounds heavier than when she had left town.

Diana was shaken at the sight of the buggy. The memories came flooding back. With a sigh, Diana drove through the stone gates that led to the house. Before she reached the house, she made the sudden decision to park her car under a magnificent white oak and walk down to the pond that served as the boundary between her father's estate and the Amish land next door—the land belonging to Jethro's family.

Diana sat on the grass and took off her shoes, letting the soft grass brush her toes. After a few moments, she lay back down, looking at the sky. If she had made a different choice all those years earlier, this would be her life now.

And was it so bad? She had loved Jethro, but could she really have taken to the Amish way of life? A life of simplicity, a life where she didn't have to rush around and meet deadlines, a life of raising children. But why was her life now any better? Sure, she earned a good living. But what did that do for her? She earned a good salary, but what did she have to spend it on? A tear formed in the corner of her eyes as she recalled the Scripture:

> Because thou sayest, I
> am rich, and
> increased with goods,
> and have need of
> nothing; and knowest
> not that thou art
> wretched, and
> miserable, and poor,
> and blind, and naked.

Yes, she had money and a nice apartment, but she didn't have friends, not really. She certainly didn't have children, and she had always wanted a big family.

Diana thought she heard the sound of a child's voice. Surely, she was imagining it. Had she lost her mind? She sat up and looked around. A young child was skipping over to the pond.

The Amish child came to an abrupt stop when she saw Diana.

Diana hurried to reassure her. "Hiya. Wie gehts?" *Hi, how are you?* She pointed in the direction of the house. "I live over there."

The little girl nodded. "What's your name?" Diana asked. "Ich bin die Diana." *My name is Diana.*

The little girl smiled but looked down at the pond.

Diana looked around for the child's parents

but couldn't see any. "Are you lost? Where's your *mamm*?"

The little girl took a step back, suddenly scared.

"It's not safe to be near a pond by yourself," Diana continued. "Will you come with me and we'll find your parents?"

The girl still looked afraid, so Diana bent down and picked up a flat stone. "Have you ever done this?" She skimmed the stone across the pond.

It had the desired reaction. The little girl giggled. Diana selected another stone and held it out to her. Hesitantly, the little girl walked forward and took the stone. Diana demonstrated how to do it again. When the little girl tried, the stone skimmed a little before sinking.

Diana clasped her hands. "*Wunderbar*!"

An angry voice rang out behind her. "What are you doing?"

She spun around to see a tall Amish man striding toward them. "Sarah, you mustn't run away like this, not down to the pond." He turned on Diana. "What are you doing, letting a child play near a pond?"

Diana was angry. "I wasn't letting her do anything!" she snapped. "And you're extremely rude for an Amish man. I was down here having some peaceful time to myself when your daughter appeared. She didn't tell me where her parents were. I was trying to gain her trust so I could take her to her mother."

Diana realized the little girl was listening to the whole exchange so plastered a smile on her face. "Well, isn't it wonderful that you've finally found her," she said in a sickly sweet voice for the benefit of the child.

The man took a step closer. "Diana?"

She peered at the man. A huge black beard covered the lower part of his face. His eyes were a vivid blue. She had known only one man with cornflower blue eyes, but they had always been smiling. These man's eyes were certainly not smiling. What's more, deep worry lines emanated from the corners of eyes.

"Jethro?" she said in a small voice.

"Thank you for helping," he said in a voice which sounded anything but grateful. He spun around and strode away, more slowly this time, so the little girl could keep up with his strides.

Diana watched him walk away. He certainly looked different these days. Gone were his boyish looks. Jethro now had a rugged appearance. His shoulders were far broader and heavily muscled, no doubt from years of hard work.

And he was married. His beard was evidence of

29

that: only married Amish men had beards.
Her heart sank. But what had she expected?
Of course, he would be married after all these
years.

She silently scolded herself for holding out a
false hope that Jethro would still be single
and pining after her. What a silly, fanciful
notion!

Diana sat back on the grass, no longer caring
for its softness, and pulled on her shoes before
hurrying back to her car. Tears ran freely
down her cheeks.

When Diana stopped the car moments later,
she dabbed under her eyes, mindful of her
mascara, and looked up at her childhood
home. It was just as she remembered it,
historic, massive, and stone, in stark contrast
to its surroundings, ancient beech trees
against a backdrop of rolling hills. Diana got
out of the car and walked past the colorful
hydrangeas, up the stairs between the

columns, and reached her hand for the antique brass knob.

"Diana!"

Diana turned around to see her sister, Allegra, running over to her. Allegra embraced her warmly.

Diana hadn't seen Allegra, or her other sister Celeste for that matter, since the previous Christmas, when they had visited with her for a few hours. Allegra looked the same as ever, supremely elegant.

"How's Dad?"

Allegra released her. "Much better. He gave us a bad scare, though. Come to the house and see him."

Diana stepped forward, but Allegra put her hand on her arm and gently restrained her. "No, Diana, the house—the Stone House."

Diana was puzzled. The Stone House was the

manager's house, far beyond the main house. She looked up to see Allegra watching her, worried.

"Dad did say he kept a lot of what happened from you, but this morning he was too weak for me to ask any questions as to how much he *had*, in fact, told you. I don't know how much you know. We were forbidden to say anything to you." Allegra paused and took in Diana's blank expression. "When you see him, please don't ask him anything. Afterward, I'll fill you in on everything."

Diana was worried but knew better than to press Allegra. Why was her father in the Stone House? Perhaps because it was on the one level, so no stairs would have to be navigated. Yet, it seemed to be more than that. Allegra seemed nervous and fidgety, whereas she was usually down to earth. Allegra was the sensible, level-headed sister, despite being a year younger. Diana had never seen Allegra nervous like this before, but decided it must be due to their father's condition.

What had their father forbidden Allegra to tell Diana? Those questions would have to wait, as Allegra clearly had no intention of explaining until Diana had seen their father.

The walk from the main house to the Stone House seemed to take forever. Although on the side of a slope, the entrance to the sprawling Stone House was on level ground, and the elevated huge deck at the front of the house afforded a wonderful view of the pastures flanked by pines and beeches.

As Diana hurried inside to greet her father, she was struck by seeing the pieces of antique furniture that had belonged to her mother. Surely, they belonged at the main house? Something was wrong.

Ethan Hunt was lying in bed, looking for all the world like a frail old man, his former vigor gone. His lips were compressed into a thin white line. Diana was horrified at how feeble he looked. It was as if she had been away for fifty years, not just ten. Waves of guilt overwhelmed her.

"Diana." The word was barely a croak.

Diana hurried over to the bed and took his hand, her tears falling freely.

"Hush, child, don't fret yourself." Ethan's eyes closed again. "I'll be okay," he managed to add.

Diana sat on his bed, wringing her hands with worry.

"He'll be fine," Allegra reassured her. "He does have to go on a strict diet now, and after he recovers he has to do some careful exercise, but he'll be okay in time."

Just then, a nurse came into the room, so Allegra walked over to the door and signaled Diana to follow. Ethan appeared to be already asleep.

Diana was confused but keen for answers. She knew from long experience that pushing Allegra for a response would get her nowhere, so she simply followed Allegra to the kitchen.

The kitchen was far smaller than the kitchen in Hawk Mountain Manor, although was bigger than the whole square footage of Diana's studio apartment back in New York.

Allegra set a cup of strong, black coffee in front of Diana, and without further ado, asked, "How much do you know?"

Diana went weak in the knees and was glad she was sitting down. "About what?"

"About the finances, about Dad selling Hawk Mountain Manor."

The room spun—everything faded. A surreal sensation threatened to overwhelm Diana. She fought back the nausea that came again and again in waves. "What? Dad is selling Hawk Mountain Manor?" she squeaked.

Allegra sighed heavily and didn't speak for a minute or two. "Diana, I'm so sorry Dad didn't tell you. He didn't want you to worry, so he swore us to secrecy."

Diana again tried to find her voice, but the words didn't want to come out. "When? When?" she sputtered.

Allegra sighed again. "I'm sorry to have to tell you all this. Our family's real estate holdings crashed. Dad nearly had to declare himself bankrupt. The Wittmer family came to the rescue. They gave a very good price for Hawk Mountain Manor."

"The Wittmer family?" Diana interrupted. "Why would the Amish want this place?"

Allegra ignored Diana's question. "The Wittmer family allowed Dad and Celeste free rental on the Stone House indefinitely. They paid Dad's medical expenses and even the nurse's fees."

"But how? I thought the Wittmers didn't have any money for a nurse, let alone for medical expenses, or even to buy Hawk Mountain Manor. This is all too much to take in at once." Diana burst into tears.

Allegra walked over and placed her hand on her arm. "I know it must be a horrible shock, and Dad's heart attack coming on top of it all wouldn't help. I'm sorry, Diana."

Diana grabbed a box of tissues sitting by the bowl of fruit and blew her nose. "Surely, they don't intend to live here?"

"They will sell the manor. As for the rest of it, they subdivided it, sold off parcels of land."

"What? That's terrible! How could they do that?" Diana's sobs grew louder. "Why would they buy it to split it up?"

Allegra patted Diana on the shoulder. "Diana, I realize this is very distressing for you, but Dad would have been in a very bad position if they hadn't bought it. The Wittmers paid market value, and even that was only just enough to get Dad out of debt. What would have happened if they hadn't paid his medical expenses? And Dad would still be in the hospital now if they hadn't paid for the nurse. We owe them a lot."

Diana struggled to catch her breath. "But I thought you've never liked the Wittmers? You know, when I..." Diana broke off and again blew her nose, more loudly this time, then took a big mouthful of coffee. It was so hot that she almost coughed it up. She dropped the cup and spilled coffee all over the granite countertop.

Allegra waved Diana to sit down and cleaned it up, poured Diana another cup of coffee, and then looked straight at Diana.

"I never had a problem with the Wittmers, Diana. If you recall, you were the one who decided. You didn't even ask for my opinion. I married for love, not money."

Diana was shocked by the vehemence of Allegra's words as well as the implication. "That's harsh! It wasn't that. How could I turn Amish? I mean, Amish don't have cell phones, or electricity or Internet. How could I live like that?"

She paused to blow her nose once more. "Aunt Evangeline and I talked about it at length and she said any marriage with Jethro was doomed to failure. Jethro and I were too different. My idea of fun isn't baking all day, wearing those plain dresses, having to do what the bishop says, or any of that other nonsense."

Allegra shook her head in obvious disapproval and set down her coffee cup rather too loudly. "Have you spoken with Jethro since you broke off your engagement?"

"No, of course not! It was sudden." Diana shook her head. "I told him I couldn't go through with being Amish, and left for New York soon after. You know that."

Allegra rolled her eyes and waved her hand dismissively. "I know you and Aunt Evangeline have always been close, but really, is she the world's greatest expert on marriage? I mean, how many husbands has she had?"

Diana held up three fingers. "Three," she said, rather unnecessarily.

"My point exactly." Allegra shook her head.

Diana was quite defensive. "Yes, but she wasn't compatible with any of her husbands. That's why she thought it was sensible that I shouldn't marry Jethro. Do you really think I could have turned Amish?"

Allegra narrowed her eyes. "If you had, your life would have been quite different now. You would have children and a loving husband."

Diana shook her head. How many times had those thoughts kept her awake half the night?

No, she had made her choice—she was a career woman living in New York. Her apartment building had everything she needed: a twenty-four-hour doorman, a massive library with a fireplace, a state-of-the-art playroom with a rock climbing wall, a fitness center, a residents' lounge with over one thousand square feet of outdoor space, as well as cold and dry storage, and on-site parking. That was much better than living on an Amish farm, covered in dirt and missing Netflix.

"Hungry?" Allegra asked over her shoulder.

"Sorry?" Diana was thrown by Allegra's sudden change of subject. "Um, no. I'm tired and I don't feel well. This has all been a shock."

Allegra abruptly switched the subject. "Are you dating anyone serious?"

"No!" Diana realized that her denial had come out too strongly.

Allegra raised an eyebrow. "Are you dating anyone at all?"

"No." This time her tone was more measured.

"Hmm," was Allegra's only reply. "I'll show you to your room."

The bedroom was much smaller than Diana's bedroom at the manor, but Diana had expected that to be the case. She was also not surprised to find that her antique Victorian era four-poster bed was missing, and in its place was a comfortable-looking but somewhat uninspiring bed.

Thank goodness her mother's quilt was on the bed. The quilt was a family heirloom. Diana, as the oldest daughter, had inherited the quilt, and it had been on her bed when she had left for New York. It was a Traditional English hexagon quilt, and had been made by her grandmother.

Diana looked at the work that had gone into

the pretty blue and lavender English patchwork quilt. It was constructed entirely from hundreds of small, hand-pieced hexagons, which were pieced together to form patchwork 'flowers.' Each hexagon was made by basting fabric to a hexagonal paper template, and then all the hexagons were hand stitched to each other. The basting and templates were then removed from inner hexagons, leaving the outer row of hexagons intact. The quilt top was edged by half flowers.

Diana's reminiscing about the quilt was disturbed by a fat, gray and white tabby cat that jumped into the middle of the quilt, opened its yellow eyes wide, and hissed at Diana.

"Tiger!" Diana made to pick up the cat, but she hissed again and ran out of the room, her thick, furry, upright tail fluffed up like she had been given an electric shock. The cat had a terrible temper. Ethan had bought her for the girls from a rescue shelter sixteen years earlier. At the time, the family had thought Tiger's temper would improve with care, but unfortunately the cat had grown more demanding and unruly with age.

Diana's old bedroom had afforded a view of the horse pastures, but this room, being on ground level, did not afford a view of much at all. At least, the room was light and airy, with a big bay window. Diana tried to cheer herself up. *It's bigger than my studio apartment*, she told herself. Yet it was far smaller than her old room at the manor, her childhood room, filled with images of prancing ponies and her show sashes from horse shows, including her prized show ribbon from years ago when she won Youth National Champion English Pleasure Junior Rider.

And what's more, Jethro is married. Diana lay down on top of the bed and cried herself to sleep.

CHAPTER THREE

The following day, things seemed no less surreal. The invitation to lunch from Aunt Evangeline had been welcome, but Diana was ill at ease and wishing she could have gone back to sleep. After waking up at five that morning, Diana had tossed and turned, unable to escape from thinking upon her troubles.

Diana sat in a pod style chair near a restful, tinkling fountain under an ancient pepper tree in the restaurant and waited for Aunt Evangeline. Having been away from home so long had made her misjudge the time for the drive, so she had arrived early. Being alone with her thoughts was something Diana wanted to avoid. She turned her thoughts to her father; at least he appeared noticeably stronger today.

Diana then forced her mind to her surroundings. The juxtaposition of willows and bougainvillea with the abundant cacti seemed incongruous, yet at the same time beautiful. *The fire pits and intimate, private dining areas would make this a lovely place for a romantic date*, she thought, but those thoughts reminded her of Jethro, so she turned her mind to the scenery.

"Diana!"

Before Diana had fully arisen from her seat, Aunt Evangeline hugged her hard and then held her at arm's length. "My dear, you've lost weight! Are you eating enough? You have dark circles under your eyes. Concealer is good for that. Aren't you wearing any make-up? We should go to Chanel and get you some blush. Their new one is just *divine*. I've missed you! Am I late?"

Diana smiled to herself. She had missed Aunt Evangeline, really the only mother she had known since her own mother, Evangeline's best friend who was nevertheless younger than Evangeline by a good twenty years, had passed away almost three decades ago.

"Let's order! I'm hungry." Aunt Evangeline's eyes glittered, and Diana knew that was a sign that Evangeline had a lot to get off her chest. "Come on, I insist you have an entrée. Lunch is my treat, after all."

Diana protested weakly. "Aunt Evangeline, I'm not hungry. I don't think I can eat much at all."

"Nonsense, my girl! Eat up! Men like women with curves, and you don't want to lose yours!" Evangeline waved an oversized hand at Diana and rearranged her ample frame into the pod chair. "I could eat a horse, and I don't intend to eat alone."

Strangely, that statement cheered up Diana, as she remembered all the times that Aunt Evangeline saying she could eat a horse had upset her when she was a child. "I could eat an appetizer, I suppose."

Aunt Evangeline looked triumphant. "And I'll have the pistachio-crusted salmon."

Diana and Evangeline made small talk until the food arrived. Evangeline watched Diana dip sourdough bread into a creamy Cajon shrimp served in a bowl, and then said abruptly, "Enough of this inconsequential small talk, Diana. I suppose you're angry with your aunt for not telling you about the decline of the family fortunes?"

Diana thought for a moment. "No, I could never be upset with you, Aunt Evangeline. It's just that it came as such a horrible shock. I had no idea. Why didn't anyone tell me? I had absolutely no idea, no idea at all." She dug her fingernails into the palm of her hand to stop the tears that were threatening to fall.

Aunt Evangeline waved a piece of sourdough bread at Diana, unconcerned that a piece of shrimp fell off the end onto the table. "Your father made me promise not to tell you. Actually, he made everybody in the family promise not to tell you. He didn't want you to worry, being so far from home, and you'd made your own life. He especially didn't want to you know about the Wittmer family buying Hawk Mountain Manor, and doubly so because of Jethro."

For once, Diana wished her aunt had not been so forthright in speech. She had no wish to bring up Jethro's name or even hear it spoken. It was a topic she preferred to be swept under the carpet, where she had been sweeping it for the past ten years.

Thankfully, Diana was saved by the waiter. She dallied over the choice between Charbroiled Lamb Tenderloin with fresh spinach, pesto wrapped in puff pastry and baked until golden, and the tasty-sounding Encrusted Halibut with garlic-mashed potatoes. She chose the halibut.

Aunt Evangeline immediately censured her. "My dear, never eat garlic unless your man is eating it too." Evangeline stabbed the menu with her stubby, ring-covered finger. "Why don't you try the roasted vegetable tower of grilled tofu, roasted Portobello, eggplant and zucchini, with charred tomato and basil coulis? I've had it here before and it's delicious."

Diana spoke without thinking. "I've never kissed a man, except for Jethro, so I doubt it'll matter if I have garlic-scented breath."

Evangeline was visibly taken aback, and Diana instantly regretted her disclosure. "Never?

What, never? Are you sure?"

"I think I would have noticed if I had kissed a man, Aunt," Diana said dryly.

"What's wrong with those New York men? Didn't they ask you out? You've never been on a date?" Evangeline's blue eyes were piercing at the best of times, and now she fixed her gaze intently upon Diana.

Diana squirmed in her seat. "Um, yes, one or two did ask me out, but they weren't my type." And Nick had never wanted to kiss her, apart from a quick peck on the cheek. Maybe, he'd found her horribly unattractive.

"What *is* your type, Diana?" Aunt Evangeline's tone was insistent, even accusing.

"Um, I don't exactly know." Diana was uncomfortable under Evangeline's scrutiny. If only the food would arrive soon to distract her aunt.

"Jethro." Evangeline almost spat the word.

"Excuse me?"

"Come on, Diana. Are you still pining after Jethro?"

"No!" Diana realized the word came out too vehemently to be believable, but could not resist adding, "He's married now, anyway."

"Aha!" Aunt Evangeline was triumphant. "You *are* still pining after him!"

Thankfully, to Diana's enormous relief, a waiter arrived with their meals, but if she thought Evangeline would be thrown off the trail, she was sadly mistaken.

"Maybe, you should have married him, after all."

Diana was astounded. "I can't believe my ears. *You* were the one who told me not to marry him. I probably would have, if not for you telling me what a bad match he was. And now are you saying he would have been a good match? And *you* were the one who said I could never become Amish—have you changed your mind?"

Aunt Evangeline's face showed no sign of concern. "I don't blame you for being shrill with me, dear. As I've always said, there are nice rich men and nice poor men, so why marry a nice poor man? I saw what your mother, my dear friend, suffered marrying your father."

"But they were in love," Diana interjected.

"Yes, but love isn't enough. Your father's extravagant ways did away with her fortune. I'm sure if she'd married a man with as much money as she had, he would've been wiser with money, and now your mother's money would be still in the family." Evangeline paused to pat Diana's hand. "Sorry, my dear, but you know I speak my mind."

Diana was uncomfortable hearing such words against her father, but then had a sudden revelation. "That's why you wished I'd married

Jethro, as I would now have my mother's property back."

Aunt Evangeline looked momentarily uncomfortable and changed the subject. "Eat up. You've barely touched your food."

Diana dutifully ate a mouthful but then had another pertinent thought. "The Wittmers *did* have money after all, and no one knew. But you also said Jethro was unsuitable as he was Amish, and that life as an Amish woman would be intolerable for me. You convinced me."

Aunt Evangeline nodded slowly. "Yes, it was because I thought the Wittmers had no money, and yes, I realize I was wrong about that, but it was more so because he was Amish. I had a close friend growing up, whose much older sister married an Amish man. She lived in an old cottage and worked hard, and she died after working her fingers to the bone. I wouldn't like that to happen to you."

"But was she happy?"

"Happy?" Evangeline seemed to think the question strange. "How could she be? She had no money. She always said she was happy and blessed, but I'm sure she was just putting on a brave front."

"Have you now changed your mind about Jethro, because you've found out he's wealthy?"

Aunt Evangeline shrugged one shoulder. "It didn't occur to me that Amish people could be wealthy. Sure, I know some of them run very successful businesses, but it didn't dawn on me before that they would actually have money." Her voice trailed away.

The sinking feeling Diana had experienced since her return to Lancaster worsened. Aunt Evangeline had been vehemently opposed to Diana accepting Jethro's marriage proposal, but now, she seemed to think the match would have been a good one. If Diana had known this ten years earlier, surely she would have married Jethro. Or would she? If she had truly been in love, would she have let herself be so easily persuaded? Yes, Diana was sure her feelings for Jethro had been rock-solid. So then, why on earth had she broken off the engagement?

Diana barely noticed her dessert arrive and did not, in fact, remember ordering it. She merely listened as Aunt Evangeline discussed the relative virtues of White Chocolate Raspberry cheesecake as opposed to Molten Chocolate Lava Cake.

What had she done?

CHAPTER FOUR

Diana awoke the next morning to hear voices and sounds in the house. She reached for her clock and saw it was 8.12 a.m. She huddled back down under the sheets but was stirred by a raised voice. Diana sat up in bed and tried to get her bearings. The voice grew louder. *Dad!*

A shock of apprehension pierced her to full alertness and she wondered if her father had taken a turn for the worse. Diana hurriedly pulled on a pair of old sweats and an old shirt and, not bothering with shoes, ran from the room to her father's, almost tripping over Tiger who deliberately ran between her legs. She was reassured when she heard her father's voice, strong, if not somewhat angry.

Ethan was half sitting up in bed. The first thing Diana noticed was that color had returned to his face, and he looked at least a decade younger than he had the day before. The second thing she noticed was that his visitor was none other than Jethro Wittmer himself.

Diana's hand immediately went to her hair, long and dark brown, and right now, a mess. Diana had steadfastly resisted the chic, trendy haircuts of New York and had kept her unruly long curls. Unfortunately, she was sure she had a major case of bed head from tossing and turning the night before.

"*Hiya*, Diana." Jethro looked stern. "I'm here to ask after your father's health."

"Hi." Diana was self-conscious and shuffled from one foot to another.

"Jethro was just leaving." Ethan's voice was gruff.

Jethro nodded to Diana and their eyes locked. The look that passed between them made Diana's heart flutter. After the momentary pause, Jethro left the room.

Diana waited until she heard the front door shut before crossing to her father's bed and sitting on it. Tiger jumped up too, and sat on Diana's knee, purring loudly. Diana stroked her gingerly, knowing that Tiger's purring would soon be replaced by the urge to bite.

"Dad, how are you feeling? You look better."

Ethan snorted rudely. "I was doing well until that Jethro Wittmer turned up."

Diana was puzzled. "But Allegra said he's helped you out a lot, given you a good price for Hawk Mountain Manor."

Ethan interrupted. "A good price! He subdivided the land and sold it off, and it's been in your mother's family for years."

Diana considered pointing out that her father was getting free rent, and had sold his land for a good price, and that he would be in a serious position now if not for the Wittmers but thought the better of it. At the same time, Diana was not happy that her mother's farm had been subdivided and sold. At least, her mother's English antique furniture had been saved. She crossed to the flame mahogany Victorian dresser and ran her hand over the barley twists on one side. Nearly all the antique furniture had belonged to her mother's mother and some of it had belonged to her ancestors.

Sitting on top of the dresser were two Victorian ruby glass luster vases. Diana had loved these as a child. She had been fascinated by the way the sunlight had been refracted from the crystal prism droplets and produced shimmering rainbows that danced along the walls. No rainbows today—the sky was overcast and the temperature was dropping. She ran her finger over the prisms. One tiny piece felt rough on the top, but she was unable to see a chip.

One of her mother's quilts hung above the dresser. It was a Log Cabin wall hanging quilt. Diana had helped her mother make it. *How old was I when I started helping with it?* Diana wondered. *Five or six, as soon as I was old enough to thread a needle.* Diana admired the work that had gone into the little rustic cabin, and the vivid blues, greens, and russets.

Ethan's voice disturbed Diana from her contemplation. "Diana? You're a million miles away."

"Sorry, Dad, I was thinking of old times. Look, it's your health that counts. Concentrate on getting better."

Ethan gave a half-hearted shrug. "I'm feeling a

bit better now. At least I've got a good excuse for not going to the Wittmers for dinner tonight."

Diana was puzzled. "Here?"

"No, at Jethro Wittmer's mother's house. Naomi Wittmer has invited you and Celeste to dinner."

"But I can't go!" Diana's voice rose sharply.

Ethan struggled to raise himself on his pillows. "You must go, Diana. We can't afford to insult them, unfortunately. I'd like to give them a piece of my mind, but I can't. I won't have Jethro calling by to ask after my health in his condescending manner, and I told him so in no uncertain terms. I don't mind having a civil conversation with his mother, but not him or his brothers."

With that, the nurse entered and Diana was dismissed from the room. Diana went to the kitchen and considered what to have for breakfast. She accepted it was inevitable that she would run into Jethro from time to time, but dinner was a bit more than she thought she could bear. She had no time alone to her thoughts, as her younger sister Celeste bounced into the kitchen.

Celeste was everything Diana was not. Her make-up was immaculate and her hair cut in the very latest style. Whereas Diana had always been curvy, Celeste had the figure of a catwalk model. She reached out her long, slender hand, sporting glittering acrylic nails, for the coffee pot.

"Diana, put down that bacon," Celeste lectured sternly. "If you didn't eat so much, you wouldn't have to worry about your weight."

Diana sighed. Celeste didn't mean to be unkind, but at times she was self-absorbed. "I don't want to lose weight, Celeste."

Celeste looked at her in disbelief. "At least

brush your hair. No wonder you're single. What if a man saw you like that?"

Diana sighed again and put the bacon back in the refrigerator. She had lost her appetite. The day had not started out well. "I dress to suit myself, Celeste, not a man."

Celeste rolled her eyes and poured strong black coffee into Diana's cup. "Sure. Anyway, you look like you need this."

"I do." Diana ran her hands through her hair and tousled it, and then yawned widely before pouring milk into her bowl of cereal.

Celeste moved around the table and sat opposite her. "What happened?"

"Dinner tonight with the Wittmers."

"Oh, that'll be fun. I can't wait!" A look of recognition dawned on Celeste's face. "That was tactless of me. Are you still suffering from that decision you made years ago?"

Diana pondered how to answer that question, but Celeste pre-empted her response. "The Wittmer brothers are cute, aren't they?"

Diana nodded.

"What a shame they're Amish. Diana, you know that your twelve quilts are all safely packed away."

"My twelve quilts?" Diana was puzzled.

"Diana! How could you forget! I thought you've been living in New York, not on some other planet! Yes, you have your twelve quilts, and your thirteenth will be your Double Wedding Ring Quilt."

How could I forget, indeed? Diana thought, her heart sinking. Tradition in these parts held that a girl had to have twelve quilts in her dowry, and then was ready upon her engagement to make the thirteenth quilt, the very complicated and difficult Double Wedding Ring Quilt.

Celeste studied Diana's expression. "Surely you've gotten over Jethro by now? It's been ten years."

Diana pushed her cereal around her plate with her spoon. "Yes." It wasn't exactly a lie, but it wasn't the truth either. "Anyway, he's married."

Celeste shook her head. "Not for the past four and a bit years."

Diana looked up, shocked. "What do you mean?"

"His wife drowned. She was skating on a pond..."

Diana interrupted her. "Not our pond?"

Celeste shook her head. "No, she was visiting her sister in another community. They were both skating, and Jethro's wife fell through the ice. Her sister went to get help, but it was too late."

Diana's hand flew to her throat. "But, the girls! How old were the girls?"

"Sarah was only a few months old."

"Why didn't anybody tell me?"

Celeste waved one hand at her. "Tell you? You told us that we weren't to mention any Amish to you. Specifically, Jethro. Don't you remember?"

"Yes, but..." Diana's voice trailed away. "And Jethro never remarried?"

Celeste chuckled. "Not yet, but maybe soon."

Diana felt as though she had been stabbed through the heart. She was totally unprepared for the pang of jealousy that pierced her more surely than any knife could. "He's remarrying?"

"Maybe, if Lavender has anything to do with it."

Diana took her cereal bowl over to the

kitchen sink. She heard her voice sound weak when she spoke. "Lavender?"

"Oh yes, I forgot you wouldn't have had much to do with them as you've been in New York for the past ten years. Do you remember them at Allegra's wedding?"

"Um, I..."

Celeste interrupted. "You know, Allegra's sisters-in-law, Larry's younger sisters, Lavender and Jessica?"

Diana turned around and shifted from one foot to the other. "Yes, of course, but not well. I've only met them once or twice. But they're not Amish."

"I'm sure they'll turn Amish for a man like that. Who wouldn't?" She chuckled. "Oh, *you*, obviously."

Diana shook her head. "Honestly, Celeste, you don't turn Amish just for a man! It's a big commitment, huge. It's a completely different way of life. You have to be baptized into the community..."

Celeste interrupted her. "Jessica and Lavender have always been interested in the Amish. Their mother was—is—Amish. She left the community on her *rumspringa,* but then returned to the community about eight or so years ago."

Diana was shocked. "She did! Why?"

Celeste shrugged. "No idea, but I figure Lavender is thinking about becoming Amish. Maybe she likes Jethro."

"But, but, hardly anybody ever becomes Amish," Diana sputtered.

"You nearly did."

"*Nearly*, and that's my point." Diana felt a spark of resentment at Celeste's lack of tact, but then realized she had virtually told Celeste that she did not want Jethro back.

And did she? Diana herself did not want to think along those lines, as she was sure she had ruined any chance with Jethro. Such thinking was too painful, and Diana did not want to look too deeply into the matter.

Was Celeste right, was Jethro going to marry Lavender? And if so, did Diana mind? Did she think she had any chance with Jethro, despite being so in love with him? There. She'd said it herself, *the L Word*.

Why was she unable to think this through clearly? Jethro was not married. If she intended to try to get him back, she had better figure it out soon enough or he would remarry, if Lavender's purported intentions were anything to go by.

The question remained: was Jethro at all interested in her? It had been ten years, and she had shunned him then. Surely, he would be resentful of her, or at the very least, no longer attracted to her.

Her thoughts were interrupted by the doorbell. Celeste looked up from her smoothie. "Diana, can you get that?"

Diana shrugged and made her way to the door.

Standing there, on the porch, was a tall, thin woman wearing a scowl.

"Who are you?" the woman snapped.

"I'm Diana Hunt. And you are?"

The scowl at once turned to a smile, but the smile did not meet her eyes. "I'm Mrs. Lori Long. You may call me Lori."

Diana's first impression was that Mrs. Lori Long reminded her of Cruella de Vil from the Disney movie, minus the furs, but then she silently rebuked herself for being unkind.

Lori extended her hand, and limply shook Diana's while regarding her with peculiar interest. "We must do lunch. Celeste and I have become firm friends."

Celeste walked over and took Lori's arm. "Where's Constantine?"

"He's right behind me."

For the benefit of Diana, Celeste explained, "Lori is Constantine Connors' sister." Prompted by Diana's blank look, Celeste added, "Constantine Connors, Dad's lawyer."

"Oh." Diana nodded. She didn't remember ever hearing about Dad's lawyer, much less meeting him.

"You were probably confused by our different surnames. Sadly, my husband passed away three years ago." Diana made to murmur her sympathies, but Lori continued, "And that left me free." She winked at Celeste, who smiled back conspiratorially.

Now, what was that all about? Diana wondered.

"I hear you work in advertising?" Lori asked.

Diana nodded in affirmation.

Lori simply murmured and looked away, a supreme lack of interest stamped all over her face.

They were still standing on the porch. A man walked up behind Lori. He was tall, well over six feet, and striking. Dark hair, a masculine, angular face with deep brown eyes, and a somewhat arrogant manner completed the picture of a commanding appearance. Diana fancied he looked like a pirate captain in an old movie.

"You must be Diana. We haven't been introduced. I'm Constantine Connors."

"Hello. Yes, you're my father's lawyer."

Constantine looked at Diana appraisingly. "Such a relief that your father's recovering so well. The Wittmers have been so good to him."

Diana was embarrassed at that, but Constantine did not appear to notice. "You live in New York, I hear? Any plans to move back here permanently?"

Diana shook her head. "It's all been so sudden. I'm not really sure at this stage."

"Perhaps we could persuade you to stay." Constantine's tone was silky, and Diana imagined he thought himself charming. She, however, felt he was no more charming than a predatory mountain lion. He eyed Diana speculatively. "You were engaged to Jethro Wittmer once, weren't you?"

Diana was horribly embarrassed. She figured her face had turned beet red. Diana knew at that point what the expression, 'She wished the floor would open up and swallow her' really meant. Her cheeks grew hotter and hotter. She had known coming home would not turn out well. If only she were back in New York.

CHAPTER FIVE

Diana had spent the day between reading, talking to her father, and cleaning. She was relieved that Lori and Constantine had not stayed long. The day seemed to drag on endlessly until it was time for the dreaded dinner with the Wittmer family.

The sun was going down over the pastures as Celeste and Diana drove to the Amish farm next door. Celeste was chattering away about the latest news of Hollywood, while Diana muttered sounds of agreement, at the same time imagining all sorts of unpleasant scenarios unfolding during the night ahead.

The Amish farm was picture-perfect, white wooden fences flanking green pastures. Diana knew that the farm was part of a 1715 land grant from Constantine Penn, Pennsylvania's founder. The farmhouse was built exactly one hundred years later. The two traditional stone and wood barns they passed on their way to the house were in keeping with the other buildings on the farm, although a new barn stood nearest the house. The Wittmer brothers' business was barn construction.

Diana's stomach clenched when she parked the car by the herb garden. The smell of mint was pervading. For some reason, Diana always associated the fragrance of mint with the Wittmer house, and that didn't help her mood as the memories came flooding back.

Diana had been dreading meeting Jethro's

mother, Naomi, again. Would she harbor resentment toward her? Diana had no idea.

Celeste shot a look at her. "Nervous?"

Diana clutched her stomach. "I'm terrified, to be honest."

"You'll be fine." With that, Celeste hurried toward the stairs, leaving Diana standing there with her turbulent thoughts.

Diana forced herself to walk to the front door.

Adam, one of Jethro's brothers, was standing at the door. "*Hullo*, Celeste." He shot Diana a wide smile. "*Hullo*, Diana. It's been a long time."

"Yes," Diana said, returning his smile, pleased Adam showed no resentment toward her.

Jethro's mother walked over. "*Wilkom*, Diana."

"*Denki*, Mrs. Wittmer." She searched Naomi's face, unable to read her expression.

Mrs. Wittmer ushered the women inside. The Amish were nothing if not hospitable.

Naomi had thought she would never be in the Wittmer house again. It hadn't changed in the ten years since she had last been there. It was just as she remembered it, the lack of decoration, the simple wooden furniture, the comfortable yet unadorned couches.

Diana sat with Celeste on a couch opposite the brothers. They all made small talk while Diana sat there nervously. Her knees shook, so she planted her heels firmly on the ground. That seemed to do the trick.

Diana wondered where Jethro was. Maybe, he wasn't coming to dinner, all because of her. The door opened and two little girls walked inside. Diana met Jethro's gaze briefly and then looked away. The little girl hiding behind him offered her a small smile. The other girl bounded over to Diana. "You must be Miss Hunt. My name is Rose. I'm a year older than Sarah. Sarah doesn't like to talk much. Some people say I talk enough for both of us."

Naomi appeared at her side. "Hush, child."

Rose walked back over to her father and took his hand. He looked at his daughter, a broad smile over his face. Oh, how she remembered that smile. She looked at his broad shoulders, his strong arms visible under his shirt, and his manly hands. She noticed the crinkled lines around the corners of his eyes. He looked older but more manly.

The smile disappeared when he looked at Diana. "*Hullo*, Diana. *Hiya*, Celeste. I'm glad you could come." He addressed that comment to Celeste.

Diana said, "Oh." *I'm an idiot*, she said to herself. *I can't seem to say a single, intelligent thing around this man. And all I could think of was, 'Oh.'*

At any rate, Jethro's daughters were delightful.

Diana wondered what Jethro's wife had been like. She also wondered why Sarah was so shy.

"Come on, girls, you can help me in the kitchen. Alle Daag rumhersitze macht em faul." *Sitting all day makes one lazy*. With that, Naomi ushered the two girls into the kitchen. Diana knew that Amish girls help out with chores from a young age.

A wave of nostalgia hit Diana as the enticing aroma of Amish baking filled the air. If she had made a different choice all those years ago, she would be here right now with Jethro and maybe children of their own.

But could she have had an Amish life for the past ten years? She was well aware *Englischers* often romantized the Amish way of life, admiring their simplicity and faith, but she knew that she had not overlooked the practical aspect. She had been raised English, and becoming Amish was no small feat, not for anybody. It was, after all, an entirely different culture. It would be like moving internationally to a different culture and living exclusively within that culture and within its rules.

And, of course, the Amish did live by strict rules. The rules were not written, but everyone lived by the Ordnung, the particular rules of that community. And, while she knew Jethro's community was nowhere near as strict as some, it was certainly a strict way of life compared with the life in which she had been raised.

The Amish had no electricity, no Internet, no cell phones. Of course, businesses were the exception. Most communities permitted computers, Internet and phones, even cell phones, for Amish businesses. Still, there was the clothing: modest, and all the same. Not to mention the lack of make-up and mirrors.

Diana was also aware that many wished to become Amish because they were dissatisfied with modern life. She, on the other hand, was far from dissatisfied with modern life: she fully embraced it.

"Diana? Dinner is ready."

Diana looked up to see all eyes upon her. She wondered how long she had zoned out. She stood up and followed her sister to the table. It was already laden with platters of pork chops, along with dishes of sauerkraut, potatoes, and apple butter. Her mouth watered at the aroma. Diana's usual fare was takeout.

"Sorry I'm late." Another tall man entered the room. He looked cheerful and flustered at the same time, and took his seat opposite Diana.

Diana saw he was the fourth Wittmer brother, Jeremiah. He had changed little in the last ten years.

"Diana, it's *gut* to see you again, after all this time." He winked at her.

Diana had always liked Jeremiah—he was easy-going and friendly. Still, Jethro's proximity made her uneasy. Electrical currents pulsated through her, leaving tingles running all through her body. She sucked in her breath sharply and hoped Jethro had not noticed.

Conversation stopped abruptly as everybody shut their eyes for the silent prayer. Diana used to wonder what was said at the silent prayer, until Jethro had told her to recite the Lord's Prayer silently. After that, she had done just that, and opened her eyes around the same time as everybody else.

As soon as the silent prayer was over, Rose piped up, "Why were you late, *Onkel* Jeremiah?"

Jeremiah's handsome face lighted up in a broad smile. "Mrs. Yoder drove her old horse over here to tell me her cat was stuck up a tree. I asked her if she had a ladder and she said she did. When I arrived at her place, she

83

couldn't find the ladder. I drove back and got mine. When I got back to her place with the ladder, she said the cat had gotten herself out of the tree. I turned around and headed back here. As soon as I got home, the bishop arrived to tell me Mrs. Yoder had called the phone in his barn and asked me to go back and have a cup of meadow tea and some whoopee pies with her to thank me. So, I had to go back. The cat took a liking to me and sat on me the whole time, and I sneezed the whole time as I'm allergic to cats."

Everyone, including Diana, laughed at Jeremiah's tale, which put her somewhat at ease.

Soon everybody—everybody else that is—was deep in conversation. Diana was at first grateful that no one had tried to include her in the conversation.

"Lavender helped me select the new horse," Naomi suddenly announced.

Diana gasped. "Lavender helped you select a buggy horse?"

Naomi nodded. "Her *grossmammi* is Amish."

Rose piped up. "*Aenti* Lavender helped me make an apple pie."

Diana was surprised. She had no idea Lavender was such close friends with the Wittmer family. "How long have you known Lavender?" She addressed the question to Mrs. Wittmer.

"Lavender's *grossmammi* is Amish," Naomi said again, which didn't exactly answer Diana's question. Diana wanted to ask more, but she didn't want to appear jealous.

Rose was still talking. "*Aenti* Lavender helps here a lot. She made these whoopie pies."

With that, Naomi left the table, nodding to the girls to help her. Diana looked around the table awkwardly, but nobody spoke until Naomi set two large Shoo-fly pies on the table, along with ice cream and pretzels. Diana hadn't had pretzels with ice cream since she had left for New York.

Her stomach churned. She had no idea Lavender was so close with the Wittmers, helping out Naomi and even helping her select a buggy horse. "So, what's your new buggy horse like?" she asked Naomi.

Rose was the one who answered. "His name is Harry. That was his name before we bought him. He's very fast." She put a hand over her mouth and giggled when her father shot her a warning look. "I talk too much," she said before putting her hand over her mouth again.

"He sounds like a nice horse," Diana said.

Naomi readily agreed. "He's a Saddlebred. He had some hoof issues, but he'd been badly shod. Lavender and I are certain he'll be fine now that his feet have been trimmed properly."

Lavender, Lavender, Lavender! Diana thought unkindly. It seemed to be the only topic of conversation at the dinner table. She had to admit she was more than a little jealous. It seemed Lavender could do no wrong. Even Jethro's children seemed fond of her.

"The Widow Yoder needs help," Naomi suddenly announced.

"We'll help her," Celeste said. "What kind of help does she need?"

Naomi set down her spoon. "Baking, mostly, and some cleaning."

"We can do that," Celeste said, leaving Diana wondering who the *we* meant.

After the meal, Naomi, Rose, and Sarah cleared the table. Diana offered to help, but Naomi refused, as Diana knew she would. Soon, they were all sitting in the living room, sipping meadow tea. Sarah and Rose were sitting politely. Amish children were generally always well behaved. Just as Celeste and Diana exchanged glances in a silent signal that it was time to leave, Sarah left her seat and sidled over to Diana. She held out her doll.

Diana didn't know what to say. Should she say it was a lovely doll? The Amish didn't encourage praise. Still, she knew she had to say something. "I like your doll," she said. "What's her name?"

"Her name's Esther," Sarah whispered.

A loud gasp went up around the room.

Sarah handed Diana the doll. "*Hiya*, Esther," Diana said to the doll, wondering why all eyes were suddenly fixed on her. "You be a good girl and do what Sarah says."

Sarah chuckled, and Diana handed the doll back to her. Celeste stood up. "Thank you for your hospitality, Mrs. Wittmer."

Naomi stood up, and smiled her first wide

smile of the evening. What's more, she smiled widely at Diana.

Celeste did not speak until they were in the car. "What was all that about?" Diana said. "Did I say the wrong thing about Sarah's doll?"

Celeste shook her head. "No, not at all. It's just that Sarah hasn't spoken since her mother's death."

"What? She hasn't spoken at all?"

"Oh yes, she's spoken, but only to her father, Naomi, and her uncles. She hasn't spoken to anybody else. She must really like you, Diana."

As Diana was thinking that over, Celeste continued. "I knew Lavender was close with the Wittmer family, but I didn't realize she was quite *that* close! She'll be married to Jethro in no time."

.

CHAPTER SIX

The next morning, Diana again was awoken by the sound of voices. It was a lovely, sunny day, but her first waking thought was her embarrassment over the events of the previous day. Her heart sank. Never had she felt so miserable. She was jealous of Lavender, and at the same time not wanting to admit the strength of her feelings for Jethro. *What good would it do?* she asked herself. *He's clearly lost all interest in me.*

Diana arose and slowly showered, letting the

soothing, hot water run down her shoulders. She walked barefoot to the kitchen, breakfast on her mind, but was forestalled by Celeste. "Don't go in to see Dad yet."

Diana's heart raced in alarm. "Why not? Has something happened to him?"

Celeste hurried to reassure her. "No, no. It's just that Lori's with him. I wanted to give them some time alone."

Diana processed the information. Since their mother had passed on, Diana had not seen her father show any interest in another woman. This was a surprise. "How long's this been going on?"

"Oh, Diana, you make it sound so sordid! Nothing's *going on*. Lori's cared about Dad for some time. She's going to stay with him while we all go out riding."

Diana groaned. She had forgotten about the riding. As much as she wanted to get back on a horse, she felt a little uneasy about spending a long ride with Jessica and Lavender.

"I wonder if Jethro will have the horses ready."

Diana gave a little start. "Jethro? Why would he be here?"

Celeste made a clicking sound with her tongue. "Honestly, Diana, sometimes I wonder if you take any notice of what's going on. The Wittmers own Hawk Mountain Manor now."

"I know that, of course," Diana began, but Celeste interrupted her.

"Jethro trains horses for various people in his community, and he keeps the horses here, in the barn. It's *his* barn now—well, the Wittmer family's barn. Whose horses did you think we'd be riding?"

Celeste and Diana walked down to the barn together. Diana had not visited the barn since she had returned home, being uneasy about the barn now being in the possession of the Wittmer family.

The scent of alfalfa and horses was like perfume to Diana. She realized just how much she had missed it. Diana walked over to pretty gray mare tied to a ring in the stall and stroked her long, silky mane. Just then, she noticed that the horse was already saddled, and Jethro Wittmer was, in fact, testing the girth for tightness. He was frowning. "Diana, check your stirrups for length."

"I'm to ride this horse?" Diana was delighted.

"Her name is Snow. Do you think you can handle her?"

Diana was affronted. "Of course."

"I meant no offense. I don't know if you've kept up your riding while away these ten years in New York. I don't know what you've been doing at all."

Diana wondered if there was a double meaning in his words, or perhaps she was just being overly suspicious where Jethro was concerned. "I've ridden from time to time," she said.

Jethro said no more, but led the mare out of the stable and handed the reins to Diana. As their fingers touched, Jethro's touch seemed to linger, Diana fancied, or was that just her imagination? At any rate, at his touch, lingering or not, tingles of electricity coursed through her. Diana looked at Jethro to see if he was registering the same effect, but he had turned his attention to a fat black gelding.

Diana patted the mare's satin neck and then led her out of the barn.

"Don't let your guard down with her," Jethro said to Lavender, handing the reins of a gray mare to her. "She's a Standardbred, off the track, but I've been riding her to help with her education, to get her to settle."

His words sparked jealousy in Diana. He seemed protective of Lavender, or was he merely being sensible? Diana looked around and saw that Celeste was already mounted on a bay mare. Celeste and Diana, being so close in age, had ridden together frequently as children, but Celeste had never displayed any interest in horse shows, preferring ballet and music. She was, nonetheless, a very good rider.

Diana lightly hopped onto Snow's back. Snow immediately pranced, and Diana loosened her reins realizing the mare disliked any pressure on her mouth. Lavender's gray mare looked unhappy about being ridden and constantly put her ears back. Diana shut her eyes just for a minute and imagined she was back home, ten years earlier.

When she opened her eyes, Jethro had vanished and Celeste had ridden up to her and was trying to get her attention. "Earth to Diana! Diana, what planet are you on? Are we going or what?"

Diana nodded assent and allowed Snow to move forward, and the four of them took off at a sedate walk through the pasture. That is, the other horses were walking sedately while Snow was prancing sideways. "Let me get her out in front, then she'll settle," Diana said to the others.

Diana was only a few paces in front and was easily able to hear the conversation between Celeste, Jessica, and Lavender. Celeste was teasing Jessica about Jethro.

Jessica seemed uncomfortable. "Honestly, Celeste, stop it—I'm dating Clint!"

Celeste laughed. "I know, but you find Jethro attractive."

"Who wouldn't? If he wasn't Amish, I'd ask him out."

Celeste laughed again. "The only thing is, is he more attracted to you or Lavender?"

"Lavender likes him," Jessica said.

Lavender was clearly annoyed. "That's not true, Jessica!"

Diana had not noticed it before, but she suspected that the two sisters were competitive with each other.

"Constantine Connors asked me out a few times, but I wasn't attracted to him at all," Celeste said, apparently oblivious to the tension between Lavender and Jessica. "I'm good friends with his sister, Lori, but Aunt Evangeline said she doesn't think he's still interested in me. I hope he's not interested, because that would make things awkward. What do you think, Diana?"

Diana was prevented from answering by Lavender's horse racing past her.

At first, Diana thought that Lavender was urging her mount at a log on the edge of the woods. Jessica and Celeste gasped in unison as Lavender's horse changed from her fast pace to a series of bucks. Lavender bounced higher out of the saddle with each bound.

As they reached the log, the horse stopped abruptly, but Lavender kept going. She flew into the air, over the horse's head as well as the log, and landed with a loud thump on the other side. Her horse came to an abrupt stop and put her head down to graze.

The other three hurried over and jumped off their horses. "Please, God, let her be unhurt!" Diana was almost as surprised by her silent prayer as she was by Lavender's accident. She couldn't remember the last time she had prayed.

Lavender was half-sitting in mud on the other side of the log, crying gently and holding her ankle. "Something spooked her," she said through her sobs. "I let my guard down with her. It's my fault."

Diana immediately took charge of the situation. "No, it's not your fault—it was an accident. Celeste, you ride back for help. Jessica, here, hold Snow too as well as Lavender's horse. Lavender, don't move and don't take your helmet off."

She handed Snow's reins to Jessica and tried to climb the log. It was surrounded by mud after the recent rain. The log itself was filthy, but Diana managed to scale it none too elegantly, and hauled herself over, landing in the mud next to Lavender.

"Where does it hurt?"

"My ankle."

Diana noted with relief that Lavender's riding helmet was still firmly fixed on her head. "Does it hurt to breathe? Did you land on your head?"

"No, I landed on my leg, and I think my ankle's broken."

Lavender's ankle was already swollen, so Diana removed her boot as gently as she could, but Lavender whimpered with pain the whole time. "Sorry, Lavender."

"That's okay, it just hurts so bad."

"It might be sprained rather than broken, but that's very painful too. I wish I had something to strap it with. Help will be here soon, we hadn't ridden far from the stables. Hang on, I'll have a go at strapping it with my scarf."

"You can't put your beautiful pink scarf around my muddy foot," Lavender objected.

Diana laughed. "I'm already covered in mud, and it's starting to rain."

Lavender laughed too, in spite of her pain. "I'm so sorry, Diana, for causing all this trouble. I think you have more mud on you than I have."

Diana strapped the ankle as best she could with her scarf. By the time she finished, the rain had stopped, but she and Lavender were sitting in a big muddy puddle.

The rescue party did not take long to arrive. Jethro and Celeste both arrived in Jethro's buggy. They ran over to the log. Jethro was white-faced and drawn. Diana had never seen him so upset. He did not even speak to her and solely addressed Lavender, questioning her and then helping her to his buggy.

Diana and Jessica were left to lead the horses back to the stables. Jessica was subdued and not at all talkative, which afforded Diana plenty of time to think. Could Jethro be in love with Lavender, after all? Surely, there was no other explanation for his behavior. Things were going from worse to worse.

By the time Diana and Jessica reached the stables, the paramedics had already taken Lavender to the hospital.

Celeste reported that the paramedics had been confident that Lavender's injury was a nasty sprain rather than a break. Jessica immediately left and drove to the hospital, leaving Celeste to attend to Jessica's horse.

"Diana, do you want me to wash Snow and blanket her for you?" Celeste asked. "You look like you've seen a ghost. Are you okay?"

"Off you go, Diana, I'll tend to Snow." Jethro walked out of the stable after attending to Lavender's horse. His expression looked less angry, but his expression was still tight. *Why is he looking like that?* Diana wondered.

Diana did not respond, so Jethro spoke again. "Diana, you're covered in mud. You'd better get cleaned up." His now far kindlier tone was itself warming her up.

As Diana murmured her thanks and turned to leave, Jethro spoke again. "You gave me quite a scare, Diana."

Diana was puzzled. "How so?" She looked up at his crinkling blue eyes and the worry lines which radiated out from the corners, and saw deep concern there.

"When the gray galloped back, from a distance I thought she was Snow. I thought she'd thrown you."

"Oh." Diana did not know how to respond, so nodded and headed for the Stone House. She was cold and dirty, but allowed herself a little glimmer of hope.

Did Jethro, in fact, still have feelings for her?

CHAPTER SEVEN

The next few days passed uneventfully and Diana was a little on edge. She had planned to spend much of her time with her father, yet Lori Long was spending more and more time with him each day. Diana considered going to the barn, but the reminder that Hawk Mountain Manor had passed out of her family was too much to bear.

Diana did not want to go back to New York just yet, despite the fact she was still paying rent on her studio apartment. There was also the fact that her leave of absence from work would soon expire. Her father was recovering well, but she did not want to leave him right away.

What's more, Diana's relationship with Celeste was growing stronger. Celeste was putting the finishing touches to an Album Quilt that was soon to be sold to raise money for charity, and she enlisted Diana's help. Diana felt renewed doing quilting again. It had been such a part of her life, and she had taken some classes in New York, but doing it again with family made her feel very much at home. There was something so heart-warming about quilting.

It was a beautiful day, Diana thought, as she drew back the drapes and looked out onto the limited scene. The view from the bedroom window was blocked by a large sugar maple tree which at some point many years ago had been planted too close to the house. The sky was a vibrant blue, and the smattering of high white clouds did not look threatening at all.

"Are you looking forward to going to the park today?" Celeste asked over their breakfast.

"Yes, I am. And you?"

"It should be a good time. Aunt Evangeline is always fun. I hope Constantine doesn't ruin things by being too pushy, though."

"What do you mean?"

"Lori told me the other week that he wanted to ask me on another date."

"Has he asked you a date before?"

"Yes, but I've always refused and I've given him the cold shoulder. He's clearly attracted to me though."

Diana thought this over. She had seen no sign that Constantine was attracted to Celeste.

Celeste continued, "Do you want to come to church with me tomorrow?"

"What? Go to church?" Diana was stunned. "Why would you want to go to church? Is there a man there you have your eye on?"

"Diana! How shallow do you think I am?"

Diana thought she had offended Celeste, but then Celeste chuckled.

"Who is he?"

Celeste did not have an opportunity to answer as there was a loud knock on the door.

Diana was surprised to see Jethro on the doorstep. Was she imagining it, or did his face light up to see her?

"*Hiya*, Diana."

"*Hullo*, Jethro." Diana grew bolder and added, "I haven't seen you around here lately."

Jethro smiled again. "It's a difficult situation.

I'm not your father's favorite person and he asked me not to visit him again."

That was news to Diana, and she was not happy about Jethro's disclosure. "I'm sorry, Jethro. I had no idea."

"That's fine. I hope you didn't think I hadn't visited because..." Jethro broke off and looked awkward. He was saved by Aunt Evangeline who appeared out of nowhere beside him.

"Hello, Jethro."

"Hello, Evangeline. How is Lavender? Is she with you?"

Lavender again. Diana was dismayed. *Just when I think Jethro is interested in me, it seems as if he does have feelings for Lavender.*

Diana was dismayed to see Constantine Connors behind Aunt Evangeline. She had no idea he was going with them; she expected that they would have met him at the park, or perhaps give him a ride on the way.

Constantine machinated things so he would sit next to Diana. Diana was none too comfortable, but thankfully had a window seat and tried to keep her conversation with Constantine to a minimum, answering his questions with one-word answers wherever she could. *Hopefully, he'll take the hint that I'm not interested*, she thought.

The park held happy memories for Diana. She used to feed the ducks there, but when she mentioned this to Evangeline, she was informed that nobody was allowed to feed the ducks these days.

"Amazing we got a parking spot so close to the entrance," Evangeline said.

"Just as well we did," Diana said. "We can't expect Lavender to walk too far on her foot."

"It's not too bad, Diana. I wouldn't have come if I wasn't up to doing some walking on it." Lavender, who was sitting next to Evangeline, the driver, looked over her seat at Diana and smiled.

"Last time I came, the entry was backed up for an hour," Constantine informed Diana.

Diana simply murmured.

Constantine was not deterred. "Yes, some say the playground equipment needs updating. I wouldn't know. I don't have kids. Not yet, anyway." He laughed and slapped Diana on the arm, and she tried not to flinch. Constantine continued, "But if I did, I'd take them to the petting zoo."

Evangeline overheard. "Constantine, we're not going to the petting zoo today. I hope you don't mind? I was thinking of Lavender's foot."

"Not at all, Evangeline. Unless Diana wants to see the animals? I could take her. They have alpacas and ponies, even goats and a pig. An alpaca tried to eat Lori's necklace. She didn't see the funny side of an alpaca wanting her necklace for a snack." Constantine laughed loudly. "Or was it a llama? Never mind. The petting zoo is free! How about it, Diana? We could do something different and meet up with the others later."

"Thanks, Constantine, but I'd like to stay with the others." *Is he ever going to take the hint that I'm not interested?* Diana wondered. *He sure is persistent.*

To Diana's relief, Aunt Evangeline did not encourage her to accompany Constantine. She appeared not to have overheard their conversation. "Let's sit at the picnic table by the fountain, that is, if you're up to walking to the fountain, Lavender?"

"Yes, I am, Evangeline," Lavender answered, and the group set off.

Diana was amused by the antics of some large ducks, but her happy mood soon dissipated when Constantine cornered her. "Don't worry if you find the signs confusing. Keep an eye out for one of the park guides. They're very helpful and a mine of information. Some of the ducks in those areas over there where people feed them—against the rules, of course —are often very aggressive. Those ones there are mallards, Diana. They are a large duck."

"Yes, I can see that." Diana did not mean to snap, but she had been doing her best to avoid Constantine. It seemed he was her self-appointed tour guide.

Constantine had not taken offense; to the contrary, he did not appear to have noticed. "It's amazing how fast those ducks can swim. Did you see the geese? Have you brought a camera, Diana?"

Diana shook her head, and then said, "Just my iPhone."

"If you want to take photos at the petting zoo but don't go inside the enclosure, you'll find that those high chain link fences that are around most of the enclosures will get in the way. It's hard to take photos of the animals without the fence getting in the way."

Constantine has an ability to state the obvious, Diana thought, again a little unkindly. To make amends for her thoughts, she decided she should speak to Constantine. "This is the first time I've felt truly tranquil since I arrived home. It's wonderful to relax amidst the beauty and diversity of this, God's creation."

Constantine regarded her thoughtfully. "Do you go to church often, Diana?"

Diana was surprised by the question. "No, not anymore. I used to go when I was a kid. Mom used to take us." Diana did not add that she had been to her own church weekly back when she and Jethro had been dating.

Constantine simply nodded and turned to speak with Aunt Evangeline.

Diana, however, was left with her musings.

Ten years ago, she had intended to marry Jethro. They had once been so close, but now she knew practically nothing about him. If Jethro was still in love with her, could she join the Amish community and become his wife? She had all but lost her faith. God was probably angry with her for leaving Jethro. She even had felt too afraid to pray, for fear that God had turned His back on her.

To Diana's dismay, Constantine soon singled her out again. "Why don't we walk over to the petting zoo? Their keepers put their food on the ground and the llamas get up to all sorts of funny antics. Maybe they're alpacas, after all," he added as an afterthought.

Diana nodded, and looked around desperately for somebody to rescue her. Celeste was oblivious to her plight, as usual. Lavender was sitting down, looking white-faced and drawn. Maybe the walk had been too much for her ankle, and the weather was getting hotter.

Diana tried her best to catch Aunt Evangeline's eye, to no avail.

Constantine stood up. "Would you come with me to see the animals?" Diana sighed and stood up. He took Diana's elbow and led her away. Diana considered pulling away but thought it rude.

It was only a short walk to the petting zoo. When they arrived, a staff member was answering questions about the eating habits of the goats, and Diana wished she could think of a question to ask, to escape from Constantine.

Constantine was still talking. "See that long line there, Diana?" He pointed to a snack stand. "The food is fairly reasonably priced here, but sometimes the lines are long."

Diana looked around urgently for Aunt Evangeline and the others. To her dismay, they were sill back at the fountain.

"Talking of food, would you do me the honor of having dinner with me tonight?"

Diana nearly groaned aloud. She had not given Constantine any encouragement at all. Rather, she had tried to give him signals that she was not interested in him. "No, Constantine, sorry, I just can't. Thank you for the invitation, though."

"What's wrong?"

"Wrong? Nothing is wrong. I just cannot have dinner with you."

"Are you seeing someone else?"

Now, that is none of your business, thought Diana. Instead, she said firmly, "Constantine, I cannot have dinner with you. I am sorry if that hurts your feelings, but that is how it is." Diana was embarrassed. She had never been in this situation before, and had no idea how to handle it.

Constantine looked tight-lipped. "Fine, if that's how you feel."

Diana was relieved, but then Constantine added, "Just let me know if you change your mind."

Diana had never met a more exasperating person. She kept her tone even as she said, "We should go back to the others." She strode away, and to her relief, Constantine made no attempt to dissuade her.

"Did the two of you have a nice time?" Aunt Evangeline asked in overly cheerful tones when they returned to the table. Diana shot her a warning look, which Aunt Evangeline probably interpreted correctly as she swiftly changed the subject to food. "You're just in time to eat."

Constantine regarded his sandwich. "This looks good, just how I like it. Did you make this, Diana?"

"No."

Aunt Evangeline raised her eyebrows at Diana's curt reply. "I made the sandwiches, and Diana and Celeste baked the apple pies."

Constantine rubbed his hands together. "Apple pies, my favorite." He winked at Diana.

On the way home, Diana made sure she sat between Celeste and Lavender in the SUV.

Aunt Evangeline briefly popped inside after she dropped them back at the Stone House. "Celeste and Diana, would the two of you have dinner with me tomorrow night?"

"I can't, Aunt Evangeline. Remember, I go to church Sunday nights?"

"Oh, I forgot, sorry, dear. What about you, Diana, any plans?"

"No other plans, Aunt Evangeline. That would be wonderful."

"Good, dear. I'll call you tomorrow to arrange it."

Diana decided that her mission for the rest of her stay would be to avoid Constantine Connors at all costs.

CHAPTER EIGHT

"Please, Diana, *please*!"

Celeste and Diana were having their usual breakfast ritual, which was usually passed in somewhat companionable silence. Today, however, was different.

Celeste took a fruitless swipe at a passing ant in frustration. "Diana, don't be smart! Have I ever asked you to do anything for me before?"

"Yes, as a matter of fact, lots of things."

"Lately?"

"Um, no. Well, you have me there."

"Do you have anything better to do?"

Diana thought it over. "No. If it's so important to you, I'll come to church, but just this once. Don't ask me again!"

Celeste leaped from her seat and ran to hug Diana. "Thanks. You'll like it, you'll see!"

Diana was not convinced. She was sure she had made a mistake in running away from Jethro ten years earlier, and was sure God was disappointed in her for it. It had eaten away her at for the last ten years. Although Aunt Evangeline had continually pointed out what the family then believed was the Wittmer family's lack of money, Diana had not broken off her relationship with Jethro as the family believed him to be poor; rather, it was because he was Amish.

Diana approached the church, butterflies in her stomach. She paused to gather courage and to sum up the building from the outside. It was unassuming and red brick.

"Come on Diana, let's get a good seat." Celeste urged Diana inside. They were early, which Diana had thought would be good as she could sit down before people wanted to speak to her, but now saw the disadvantages as Celeste wanted to sit up the front.

"Celeste, can we sit down the back?" she pleaded.

Celeste shook her head, but finally they compromised and the sisters took seats in the middle section.

Diana studied the church. The pale blue carpet set a serene contrast to the gold walls. The pulpit was of heavily carved wood. The whole ambiance was relaxed and friendly, whereas the church her mother had taken her to when she was a child had a forbidding atmosphere about it. Several strangers sat in the seats in front and turned around to introduce themselves. *It's not so bad, after all*, Diana thought.

Soon the music started, and Diana recognized some of the uplifting hymns. A man stood up and made announcements, and Diana's mind wandered to Jethro. Soon she would have to return to work, but how could she, when her former feelings for Jethro kept resurfacing. More and more, she was coming to realize that they had never really left and she would have to do something about them.

But did Jethro still have feelings for her? Or was he interested in Lavender, whom Diana could see sitting up near the front with Jessica? Or maybe he wasn't interested in *Englisch* women at all—why would he be? Any marriage between an *Englischer*-turned-Amish woman and an Amish man would be problematic.

The Pastor walked over to the pulpit up to begin the sermon. After greeting the congregation, he said, "Now please open your Bibles to Romans Chapter Eight."

The Pastor preached on forgiveness as well as compassion, and said that no one could separate us from the love of God. He read the first four verses of Romans Chapter Eight.

> *"There is therefore now no condemnation for those who are in Christ Jesus. For the law of the Spirit of life has set you free in Christ Jesus from the law of sin and death. For God has done what the law, weakened by the flesh, could not do. By sending his own Son in the likeness of sinful flesh and for sin, he*

condemned sin in the flesh, in order that the righteous requirement of the law might be fulfilled in us, who walk not according to the flesh but according to the Spirit."

It was just what Diana needed to hear. The Pastor preached that there is no one who is righteousness in the sight of God, and that we all think we have fallen short of Him and His ways. He said that such thinking keeps us away from God, and God does not want that.

Diana felt a load lift off her right then and there. God loved her. God was not angry with her or resentful that she had abandoned Jethro ten years earlier. She had distanced herself from God for all those years due to her guilty conscience, a guilty conscience which had built a rift in her relationship with God.

She had listened to man, not to God, in being so persuaded by Aunt Evangeline. Tears fell down her face freely.

The Pastor then did an altar call. "Is there anyone here who wants to know Jesus? Please come to the front and someone will say the Sinner's Prayer with you. Or is there anyone here who wants to renew their relationship with God? Please come forward." The Pastor motioned to the musicians to play, and they all played an old hymn. Diana recognized the words.

> *Softly and tenderly Jesus is*
>   *calling,*
> *calling for you and for me;*
> *see, on the portals he's*
>   *waiting and watching,*
> *watching for you and*
>   *for me.*
> *Come home, come home;*

ye who are weary come
home;
earnestly, tenderly, Jesus is
calling,
calling, O sinner, come
home!

Fresh tears fell. Diana decided to go forward, but was a little hesitant. It was the words of the next verse which made her stand up.

Why should we tarry when
Jesus is pleading,
pleading for you and for me?
Why should we linger and
heed not his mercies,
mercies for you and for me?

Diana squeezed past Celeste, and did not even register Celeste's surprised face. Celeste seized Diana's arm and whispered, "Would you like me to go out with you?"

Diana shook her head and walked to the front, alone. She was aware of many eyes on her, but knew they were supportive eyes.

After Diana returned to her seat, the people behind her patted her on the back, and the people in front of her turned around and shook her hand again.

The service ended soon after, and Celeste introduced Diana to several people. The Pastor came over and congratulated Diana for recommitting her life to God.

"Your sermon really touched me, Pastor."

The Pastor beamed at her and shook her hand warmly. "If you don't mind me asking, had you been under condemnation for something you had done?"

Diana nodded. "Yes, I made the wrong decision ten years ago, and I felt distanced from God over it."

At that point Diana looked up and saw Jessica

and Lavender standing next to the Pastor. They were speaking to each other, and their backs were to her, but they could not have been more than five feet away. Had they heard what she said?

CHAPTER NINE

Diana had stayed on with Celeste about ten minutes after the service and had been made to feel very welcome.

Aunt Evangeline had called around midday to invite Diana to a restaurant that night. Diana had assumed she would be giving Aunt Evangeline a ride or vice versa, but Evangeline asked Diana to meet her at the restaurant.

When Diana arrived at the restaurant, she found it an unusual mixture of styles. The outside of the restaurant screamed sophistication and elegance, yet the interior was unusually casual. The heavy, cream brocade drapes presented a strange contrast to the large prints of black-and-white farming scenes hung on every available wall space.

The waiting area was entirely gold and red with dramatic black and glass panels, and the gold patterned chairs were heavily brocaded, yet the lighting was modern.

An obsequious waiter ushered Diana to her table on the Tuscan style garden patio. The tables were not too close together, and were spread out in a beautifully landscaped and very pretty flowery courtyard. Several people were sitting around, chatting amiably. Diana was glad she was seated out here, instead of in the interior of the full-to-capacity restaurant. She far preferred open air, moonlight dining to the lavishly decorated interior.

While admiring the cerulean blue and white color scheme outside, Diana realized that the table was set for three. *Probably a mistake*, she decided. Her thoughts turned to Jethro. There was no denying it—she still was head over heels in love with him. He had felt the same way once; was there any chance he still felt the same way about her?

Just then, there was a movement at the corner of her eye and she looked up to see Constantine Connors entering the garden patio. Diana tried to look downward, hoping he would not notice her. Nevertheless, he headed straight for her.

"Hello, Diana, you are looking more beautiful than ever. How are you on this fine night?"

"Good, thank you." Her reply was curt.

To her dismay, Constantine sat down.

"Constantine, sorry, but I'm expecting someone."

"Yes, Evangeline, and me."

Diana was unable to keep the shock of her face. "What? Aunt Evangeline didn't tell me you were coming too."

"Didn't she?" Constantine laughed. "Well, this must be a lovely surprise for you."

Not likely, Diana thought, *quite the opposite. What am I going to do now?* "I'll call her and see how far away she is." Diana called and called, but Evangeline did not pick up. It went straight to voicemail each time.

By the time the waiter arrived to take their order, Diana realized to her dismay that Aunt Evangeline had decidedly set her up. She had always considered Aunt Evangeline a wise woman of good counsel, which is why she had been persuaded to abandon her relationship with Jethro ten years ago. Now, Aunt Evangeline was again interfering in her relationships, this time trying to play matchmaker, and had selected Constantine Connors for her.

Diana was at a loss. She wanted to leave at once, but decided such a course of action would be quite rude. She decided to wait for Aunt Evangeline, and then leave at the earliest opportunity.

Tonight, Constantine was nowhere near as pushy as he had been the day before and was doing his best to be charming. While this came as a relief to Diana, she much preferred to be somewhere other than in his company.

Diana tried to steer the conversation to neutral ground. "I hope Aunt Evangeline will be here soon. I can't imagine what's keeping her."

Diana meant this as a hint to Constantine that she did not want to be alone with him, but he appeared nonplussed. "Any plans to go back to New York?"

"Yes, of course. I just don't know when at this stage."

"Perhaps *somebody* could influence you to stay."
Constantine winked.

Diana tried not to shudder. "Dad's getting
much better, but he's asked me not to leave
quite yet. I do have to return to work fairly
soon, and get back to my apartment."

Constantine moved his chair a little closer to
Diana. "Anyone special over there?"

Diana was annoyed by the question and had
no idea how to respond, so she changed the
subject. "Did you see the long, glass wall
inside the restaurant? The diners can see the
chefs at work. What a novel idea. It's an odd
mix of styles in there, isn't it? I wonder where
Aunt Evangeline could be. I was looking
forward to dinner with her."

Diana's chattering was stopped by
Constantine placing his hand over hers. Diana
was so shocked by his move that she did not
immediately pull her hand away. Just then, she
felt eyes boring into her and looked up, and to

her horror, Jethro was staring straight at her. The surprise in his eyes was unmistakable. He was accompanied by Jeremiah, Adam, Ezra, and several other Amish men.

Diana was sure that the Wittmer brothers had all seen her, but they did not catch her eye as they moved away to a far table. *They must think I'm having a romantic dinner and don't want to disturb us*, Diana thought with a sinking heart. It was only then that she snatched her hand away.

"My dear Diana, I can see I make you nervous and for that I apologize." Constantine was going to say more, but thankfully, Aunt Evangeline arrived.

"Sorry I'm late. Have you two gotten acquainted?"

Diana narrowed her eyes and looked daggers at Evangeline. Clearly, the tardiness was all part of Aunt Evangeline's matchmaking plan. "I'm looking forward to a private word with you later, Aunt Evangeline," Diana said sternly.

Aunt Evangeline actually winced at her tone.

Constantine spoke conspiratorially. "Don't look now, Evangeline, but those Amish men are here too." He giggled in a most unmanly way.

Aunt Evangeline turned around to look.

"No, Evangeline, I said not to look." Constantine giggled again.

"Oh, the Wittmer brothers?" Evangeline asked.

"Yes, Jeremiah, Adam, Ezra, and Jethro."

Diana was annoyed. "Constantine, they are good, Godly men. It's not nice to make fun of people."

For the first time since she had known him, Constantine looked surprised. "I didn't know you were a goody-goody-two-shoes, Diana!"

Diana stood up. "Excuse me, Aunt Evangeline and Constantine. I have to leave. I look forward to talking to you later, Aunt Evangeline," she added pointedly.

Aunt Evangeline had the dignity to look guilty. "I'll walk you out. Excuse me for a moment, Constantine."

Evangeline and Diana did not speak until they reached the car, apart from when Diana offered to pay but Evangeline would have none of it. "Aunt Evangeline, what were you thinking?"

Aunt Evangeline furrowed her brow and wrinkled her nose. "You don't like Constantine?"

"No, I don't!" Diana said quite firmly. "He's been making advances at me ever since I've met him. He's overly familiar with me despite me not giving him the *tiniest* amount of encouragement. To be quite frank, I find him creepy. Creepy! Plus you got me here under false pretenses. I'm quite upset about it all. I was looking forward to having a nice dinner with you, too."

Aunt Evangeline looked crestfallen. "I'm sorry, Diana. He's a good catch, and as you don't seem at all successful in the dating department, I thought I'd give you a helping hand."

"I know you were only trying to help, but he really isn't my type." Diana was too kind to add that she'd once been in love, but Aunt Evangeline's interference had caused that to end. However, Diana had accepted the fact that it was entirely her own responsibility in accepting the bad advice.

"Aunt Evangeline, I do love you, and I'm grateful that you want to help, but please promise me you won't try to help me with my dating life again?"

Evangeline was clearly contrite, and duly promised.

On the drive home, all Diana could think about was Jethro's sad face. It occurred to her that Aunt Evangeline's interference might have ruined her relationship with Jethro a second time, and there was nothing she could do about it.

CHAPTER TEN

Diana stood outside the cafe window on a sunny morning the following day, her mouth watering at the sight of the tempting pastries. She had decided to have the day to herself, to clear her thoughts. It had been relaxing wandering idly past the stores, window shopping and enjoying the cool breeze. Diana usually tried to eat well but occasionally treated herself, and today seemed like a good day for a treat. Lots of sugar would go a long way to soothing her aching heart. Had she lost Jethro forever?

The store window was enticing, with its range of fresh bread, cakes and pastries, chocolates, coffees, imported teas, and condiments. Diana decided to have a coffee, but what to eat? The choice would be difficult.

Diana went inside and surveyed the surroundings. The little café was warm and inviting, just the place to relax for half an hour or so, and think things over. Even the walls were the color of food; the decor was all honey and chocolate brown.

Diana narrowed it down to a choice between an Amaretto, a dome-shaped cake which a handwritten card informed her comprised three layers of Italian sponge cake filled with layers of creamy vanilla custard, baked in a sweetened almond paste, and Babas, Italian spongy pastry with a very generous filling of oozing vanilla custard. She had decided on the unusual looking Amaretto when her gaze fell upon the Dark Chocolate Ganache. The card described it as two layers of light chocolate sponge cake filled with chocolate mousse, covered with rich, dark chocolate ganache and topped with a drizzle of white chocolate. Decisions!

"Diana? Diana Hunt?"

Diana turned around to look into a familiar face. "Abigail Fischer?"

"Yes, how are you? It's Abigail Briskey now."

"Good, and you? I haven't seen you for years. I almost didn't recognize you without your Amish clothes. Didn't you move away and get married? And, you're no longer Amish?"

To Diana's consternation, Abigail started crying. "I'm sorry."

Diana did not know what to say, especially when Abigail's tears showed no sign of letting up. "Abigail, would you like to sit down and have a coffee? I've just ordered one and I was about to order cake. My treat. I'm here from New York for a short time and I'd love to catch up. Unless now isn't a convenient time for you?"

Abigail merely nodded, her tears flowing freely as she sniffed into a tissue. Diana put her arm around her shoulders and led her to a seat. "Coffee?"

Abigail just shrugged so Diana went to the counter and ordered her a latte, and hoped Abigail was not dairy intolerant. Diana ordered a Dark Chocolate Ganache as well as a White Chocolate Mousse Slice, described on the handwritten card as having layers of rich European chocolate cake filled with layers of white chocolate mousse, and topped with whipped cream, chocolate syrup and shavings of dark Swiss chocolate. Abigail could choose one, and she would have the other.

After paying, Diana sat down opposite Abigail. The hard wooden chairs upholstered in a pale caramel color were pretty but uncomfortable, and the wooden table was not quite the right height.

Diana contemplated what to say, but Abigail spoke first. "I'm sorry, Diana. Lately, I think I'm fine, but then I just start crying."

"What's happened?" Diana wedged a little piece of paper under one of the table legs to stop it rocking.

"It's my husband, Landon. He passed away five months ago."

"Oh Abigail, I'm so sorry."

Abigail nodded. "I decided to become English when I was on my *rumspringa*, and not long after I met my husband, Landon. After he died, I came back home to be with my parents, to get away. It's all so hard. I'm sorry, Diana, what must you think of me? We haven't seen each other for years, and here I blurt out all my troubles to you."

"Oh, not at all."

Abigail abruptly changed the subject. "So, I heard you were living in New York. How long have you been back?"

"Only a week or so. Dad had a heart attack, but he's doing well now."

"I heard. I knew all about, well, you know."

Diana assumed Abigail was referring to her father selling the family property to the Wittmers, but had no chance to respond as the coffees were served.

"I just guessed and ordered you a latte, Abigail. I hope you're not dairy intolerant."

"Oh no, that's fine, I'm not. Thanks, Diana." Abigail skimmed the small amount of froth off the top with her spoon and ate it. "Sorry to bring that up, Diana. You look sad."

"It's all been a bit of a shock. I had to race back from New York with Dad being ill, and I had no idea that Hawk Mountain Manor had been sold until I arrived."

"Oh no, Diana, that would have been awful!"

"It was." The cakes arrived, and Diana took the opportunity to wedge another bit of paper under the stubbornly offending table leg. "I got two different cakes as I didn't know which one you'd like. You choose the one you want, and I'll have the other."

"Oh, I couldn't. You choose."

After some good-natured banter, Diana ended up with the White Chocolate Mousse Slice, and Abigail with the Dark Chocolate Ganache.

Abigail sipped her coffee before speaking. "It must have been hard to give up Hawk Mountain Manor, but it's helped a lot of people."

"How so?" Diana was puzzled.

"Didn't your father tell you?"

Diana shook her head, bewildered.

"Well, it's not public knowledge. You would know that the Wittmers split up the land around Hawk Mountain Manor. Anyway, they sold off everything but the house complex and ten acres around it. They donated the money for the rest to several charities that target poverty, one of which I used to work for."

"I had no idea!" Diana said, and then asked, "You don't still work for the charity now?"

"No, but that's how I knew all about it, as Jethro's involved with that charity. I've always stayed friends with this community. The Wittmers have helped me a lot since Landon died." Abigail sniffed again.

Diana figured the best thing to do for Abigail was to let her unburden herself, so tucked into the chocolate cake and waited for Abigail to speak.

"I'm sorry to tell you all this," Abigail continued. "I know we weren't close friends, but you were always nice to me."

"I'd like to be your friend now, Abigail. Besides, I don't have any friends these days. I mean, not even really back in New York. I've been a bit of a loner these last years."

Abigail beamed. "I could really do with a friend right now, too. It's been hard, moving back with my parents, but with no money…" Abigail broke off. "It's a bit embarrassing."

"No, seriously, go on if it helps."

"Did you know anything about Landon, my husband?"

Diana shook her head.

"He was in business, but he was swindled out of his money. A partner bought into the business, and Landon thought he was wonderful. He was very persuasive. Turns out he was a con man. He took us for everything;

we ended up bankrupt. Landon found out the night he died; he was driving over to his partner's house to confront him. The police said he was driving too fast, and he veered off the road on the ice and hit a tree." Abigail dabbed at her eyes.

"Could they do anything?"

"The police?" Abigail shook her head. "No, the con man was too clever. He's a lawyer; he had everything tied up. We'd mortgaged the house to the business and it was sold to pay off the debts. Constantine had been too clever for Landon."

The hair stood up on the back of Diana's neck. "Constantine? What's his last name?"

"Connors. Constantine Connors."

Diana went cold all over. "Abigail, I know him! He's asked me on a date. Personally, I've found him really quite distasteful and I haven't given any encouragement, quite the opposite in fact, but he won't give up."

Abigail looked horror-stricken. "Diana, I don't mean to be rude, but do you have any money? I mean, are you wealthy? You're obviously an attractive woman, so please don't take this the wrong way, but this man is all about calculated self-interest and deceit. He would only pursue a woman, any woman, if he thought money was involved."

Diana laughed softly. "No, I'm just an advertising executive. The pay's okay, but it's expensive living in New York. I only live in a tiny studio apartment. I do save a lot of my pay, but I'm not a wealthy woman."

Abigail looked puzzled.

Diana added, "But you do have something there. His pursuit of me *is* very strange."

"Could he possibly think your family is

wealthy? Would he think you still own Hawk Mountain Manor?"

"No, he's Dad's lawyer."

Both girls looked shocked and stared at each other.

Diana gasped. "How silly of me. I didn't think of that until now. There's definitely more to this."

Abigail nodded agreement. "Do you have an inheritance?"

"No. Not now, anyway. Not now that Hawk Mountain Manor has been sold and Dad has no money."

Abigail shook her head. "What about a Trust? Your mother's family was the one with the wealth. Did your mother leave you any money in a Trust Fund? You girls were young when she passed. Do you know anything about her will?"

"No, but I'm over twenty-one now, and no one's ever mentioned a Trust Fund."

Abigail pushed her cake around her plate with her fork. "I don't know anything about the law, but I've only heard of Trust Funds set to be collected, or whatever the term is, when the person turns twenty-one or twenty-five. And you're well over that age now." She offered a weak laugh. "No offense."

Diana rubbed her forehead vigorously and sighed. "It's been one surprise after another since I got back. I haven't heard any whisper of a Trust Fund, but it would certainly explain Constantine's behavior, especially as he apparently pursued Celeste first, and then me. Plus his sister, Lori, is clearly interested in my father."

Abigail set down her empty latte glass. "If any sort of money is due to come to you, that would make perfect sense, as Constantine would know about it."

155

Diana thought things over. "Like I said, there's never been any hint of it, though. I'll have to ask Dad. I can't understand why he and Aunt Evangeline would have kept it from me. I suppose there's no use speculating, I'll have to ask Dad outright." Diana groaned aloud.

CHAPTER ELEVEN

Diana slipped in to check on Ethan, as was her custom each time she arrived back at the Stone House. This afternoon he was looking much stronger and was sitting on a chair propped up by cushions, with his feet on a rest. Although sunlight was streaming into the room, the atmosphere in the room was decidedly gloomy. Even Tiger, who sat at Ethan's feet, looked subdued.

Diana pondered whether it was the right time to bring up the matter of a Trust Fund.

Ethan was a stubborn man with a quick temper, and today he was snapping at his nurse.

Diana threw the nurse sympathetic looks, and the nurse smiled back. She did not seem offended. No doubt, she was well accustomed to cantankerous patients.

Ethan started to rise from the chair, and the nurse tried to prevent him.

Diana intervened. "Dad, you're supposed to be resting. Do what you're told and sit back down."

"I'm not a child, Diana, and everyone is treating me like one!" Ethan's tone grew more belligerent.

"Here, Dad, drink your coffee." Diana handed him the steaming mug and a cookie.

Ethan took one bite and nearly spat it out. "That cookie tastes disgusting."

Diana sighed. "It's low fat and low sugar. It's good for you."

"Yes, and that's why it tastes disgusting." Ethan slammed the cookie down, causing bits of it to break off and fall to the floor. Tiger pounced on a piece and ate it. "I'm not going to eat it. I'd rather be dead if I have to eat food like that."

Diana sighed, and bent down to scoop up the broken bits of cookie, avoiding annoyed swipes from Tiger's paw. *For someone who doesn't want to be treated like a child, he sure is acting like one,* Diana thought. "You don't mean that, Dad. What would we do without you?"

"You've done well enough without me for the last ten years!"

Diana tried not to be hurt. She knew it was just Ethan's manner, and he was recuperating after a life-threatening heart attack. The nurse left the room, and Diana decided that now was as good a time as any to bring up the question of a possible Trust Fund. After all, she doubted Ethan's mood would improve anytime soon.

"Dad, can I ask you something?"

Ethan merely grunted between sips of coffee.

Diana took a deep breath, and launched into her questions. "This might be a strange question, but is there a Trust Fund for me?"

Ethan's reaction was intense. He jerked, and spilled his coffee. Diana hurried over to mop it up.

"Don't fuss."

Diana sat back down and waited for Ethan to answer. When he didn't answer but kept sipping what was left of his coffee, Diana knew that something was going on.

"Dad, is there a Trust Fund?"

"Who told you that?"

"Dad, it's a simple question. Is there or isn't there?"

"Don't take that tone with me, child." Ethan's face turned a deep shade of beet red.

Diana did not want to upset a patient with a heart problem, so decided not to pursue the matter. She considered instead seeing a lawyer. She looked up at Ethan, but he had set down his coffee mug and was asleep—or was pretending to be.

What next? Her father's reaction gave her cause to believe that there was in fact a Trust Fund, or at least something similar.

There was an old desktop computer in the living room, and Diana knew it was hooked up to the Internet as she had daily checked her Facebook and Twitter accounts on it.

Diana crossed to the sturdy, antique English Oak desk and fondly ran her finger over the grain, admiring the mellow patina of amber hue. This had been one of her mother's favorite pieces of furniture. It had three frieze drawers and three additional drawers on each side with tramline carvings and brass drop handles. When Diana was a child, the central drawer had been lockable but the key was long since lost. The old desktop computer looked incongruous sitting on top of a valuable antique, although it looked as worn as the black leather top on which it was perched.

Diana settled into the uncomfortable lumpy chair, also an antique. Her mother had been proud of this chair. Made in 1875, it had been owned by her mother's great grandfather who was a captain in the British navy. The velvet upholstery was an unfortunate shade of salmon pink.

A search for 'Trust Fund' brought up too much information. Where to start? After ten or so minutes, Diana found what she was looking for. If she did have a Trust Fund coming, it would be what was known as a *testamentary trust.* To her alarm, the web page said that a trustee is appointed to direct the Trust until the time that minor beneficiaries reach the specified age and are capable of fending for themselves, or achieve an educational goal, or get married.

What if Constantine Connors was the trustee? The web page said it is often very difficult for beneficiaries to bring successful action against a dishonest trustee. It added that such action is slow, time-consuming, and expensive, and even then does not always succeed.

Diana then found another website, which said that the trustee is supposed to oversee the Trust for its duration. Constantine would have been too young to be a trustee at the time her mother would have set one up. He would have been a child or a teenager at the latest when the Trust was set up, assuming that there was one. *I'm getting ahead of myself here*, Diana thought. *There might not even be a Trust Fund at all.*

Diana called Allegra, but there was no answer. As she was trying a second time, Celeste came home. "How was your morning?"

"I ran into an old friend of ours, Abigail Fischer, but her married name is Briskey."

"Abigail? Didn't she leave town while on *rumspringa?*"

"Yes, and she got married, but her husband passed away recently."

Celeste nodded. "Poor Abigail!" She fell silent for a moment, and then asked, "Hungry?"

"No! I'm overloaded with chocolate cake. I couldn't eat another mouthful."

Celeste merely snorted. "Lucky thing. Want to talk to me while I get some lunch?"

"Sure. I could probably manage another coffee."

Diana followed Celeste through the living room into the kitchen, and took a seat. "Celeste, have you ever heard anything about us girls having a Trust Fund?"

Celeste all but shrieked. "What? We have a Trust Fund?"

"No, well, I don't know. Maybe. Abigail said something that made me think we did, and when I asked Dad, he got angry and wouldn't tell me."

Celeste stopped spreading the bread and put down her knife. "What did he say?"

"Nothing. He didn't say anything. I asked him straight out if there was a Trust Fund and he refused to answer, and then got quite angry, and then he pretended to fall asleep so I couldn't ask him any more about it."

Diana had Celeste's attention now. "That *is* strange. Have you asked Allegra?"

"I've tried to call her, but it goes straight to voicemail."

Celeste scratched her head and then resumed spreading the bread. "But doesn't somebody get the money or property, whatever, when someone turns twenty-one? We would have had it by now."

"No, I was just googling it before you came home. It's usually twenty-one or twenty-five, but sometimes the terms state that it gets paid when someone gets married or something like that."

"Well, Allegra's married."

Diana shrugged, and poured herself and Celeste a coffee each.

"Thanks for that. Have you asked Constantine?"

"No, and I don't want to. Celeste, he's been pursuing me lately." Diana hoped Celeste would not be offended or hurt as Celeste had told her that Constantine had previously pursued her. She carefully studied Celeste's expression, which to her relief was one of nonchalance.

"And you're not interested?"

"No!" Diana said, a little too vehemently, and then added, "You told me the other day that he'd earlier been interested in you?"

"Yes, I found him a little persistent really but harmless. He kept asking me out, called me all the time. I would have been blunt with him at the beginning only for being friends with Lori. Finally, I did have to be very blunt with him, as he was getting quite bothersome."

"So you were never interested in him?

Celeste shuddered and rolled her eyes. "Not hardly. But he's Dad's lawyer, so he'd know about the Trust Fund, if there *is* one, of course. Why don't you want to ask him?"

"Celeste, I'm wondering why he was so

persistent with both of us. If there *is* a Trust Fund, it occurred to me that he might think it was his way to easy money. I only found out recently that he's a con man, and he did trick someone I know out of a large sum of money and send them bankrupt, but that's just between us. I don't want that to get back to Lori."

Celeste slapped her half-eaten sandwich down on the countertop. "Seriously? Now you have me worried. What are we going to do? If this is true, then I'm worried about Lori's friendship with Dad. I used to think of her as a friend, but lately it's dawned on me that she was just using me to get to Dad. But would Mom have left us enough money for them to want to get their hands on it?"

Diana held up her hands and shrugged. "I could be wrong about the whole thing. Mom's family was very wealthy, and as much as she loved Dad, she knew only too well about his spending, and she might've put something away for us in her will. It's all guesswork, though. The first thing I have to figure out is who her lawyer was back then."

Celeste picked up the remains of her sandwich and chewed it thoughtfully. "Aunt Evangeline would know."

"Aunt Evangeline!" Diana slapped herself on the forehead. "Of course! Why didn't I think of that? Aunt Evangeline would know about any Trust Fund too. She was Mom's closest friend!"

Celeste picked up her cell phone and handed it to Diana. "Call her now and ask her."

Diana took the phone. "Celeste, I think this needs to be done in person. I'm going to drive over to her place now. Do you want to come?"

"Yes, but let me change first. I won't be a minute. Can you bring the car around? I left it at the barn." Celeste tossed the car keys to Diana. "And don't call Aunt Evangeline, or she'll want to know why we're coming. We need to take her by surprise."

"What if she's not home?"

"No harm, no foul. It's better to take the chance. At least we'll have been for a nice drive. Do you have anything better to do?"

Once again, Celeste had a point.

CHAPTER TWELVE

Diana hurried out the front door and charged into Jethro. She only had time to throw up her hands to protect herself, and they landed on his chest, which Diana noted was hard and muscled. The familiar tingles of electricity ran through her, so she snatched her hands back as if burned and jumped backward, and then immediately regretted it when an unmistakable look of hurt passed across Jethro's face.

Jethro stood looking down at her, and neither

spoke. Diana held her breath until she felt she would burst. It was Jethro who broke the silence. "Diana, are you all right?"

"I was rushing out to get the car." Diana was annoyed to hear her voice come out breathlessly.

"On the way to see anyone in particular?"

Was Diana imagining it, or was there a hint of concern, or even jealousy, in Jethro's voice?

"Celeste and I are going to see Aunt Evangeline."

"Oh." Jethro's monosyllable was followed by another uncomfortable silence.

This time Diana was the first to speak. "Ethan's awake. Go right through."

"No, Diana, I've come to see you."

Diana was taken aback. "Me?"

Just then, Celeste rushed out, and with a, "Hi,

Jethro! Diana, you didn't get the car!" seized Diana's arm and guided her down the gravel driveway toward the car.

What did Jethro want to speak with me about? Diana's stomach was churning. When she reached the car, she hopped inside and fumbled with the key. She sat there without starting the car, and took a few deep breaths.

"This Trust Fund matter is really upsetting you, Diana." Celeste's voice held concern.

"What? Oh, I'm shaken up by everything, I suppose." *And particularly now that I have no idea what Jethro was going to say to me. What on earth could it be?* Diana's stomach continued to churn.

As Diana put the car into reverse, she felt someone watching her, and looked up to see Jethro standing along the pathway, looking at her. Diana let out a deep sigh and drove off.

The drive to Aunt Evangeline's somewhat

soothed Diana's nerves and settled her stomach. Having to concentrate on not getting lost was taking her mind off her problems, and the scenery was magnificent.

"Celeste, this isn't looking too familiar. You'd better navigate from here on in."

"Do you want to pull over and I'll drive?"

"No, I'll be all right, but tell me where to go. I thought I'd remember, but it looks a bit different."

"You're okay, you're on the right road. Stay on this road a bit. Diana, are you sure you're okay? You've been acting anxious since we left the house."

"Jethro said he wanted to tell me something."

"Oh, he probably just wanted to tell you that he's engaged. Turn right onto Prospect Street."

Diana's stomach muscles clenched, and she felt dizzy.

"Diana! Turn now, quickly!"

Diana only just made the turn. "Jethro is engaged?" Diana felt as if she would pass out. Tears pricked at the corners of her eyes and threatened to fall.

"Take the next right."

"Celeste?"

"What?"

"You said Jethro is engaged?"

"How would I know what he wanted to tell you? I guessed he must be engaged and wanted to tell you because you two were once engaged. Diana, are you listening?"

Diana nodded. She didn't trust herself to speak. The tears threatened to flow, this time from relief, but Diana counseled herself that relief might be premature as perhaps Jethro was, in fact, engaged. She had no idea why he would want to speak with her.

Celeste was still directing. "Turn left at the stop sign."

"Yes, I remember from here now."

Aunt Evangeline's home was a spectacular home. To the right were trees overhanging the entrance, which was an ornate gateway to a courtyard and the only area of the front, apart from the garage, which did not have thick trees in front.

Celeste and Diana walked down the paved pathway flanked by lush trees and even thicker grass. When Aunt Evangeline did not answer the door, Diana tried calling her again, but again it went straight to voicemail. Celeste and Diana looked at each other.

"What will we do?" Diana asked.

Celeste thought for a moment. "Surely, she can't be too far away. Call again and leave her a message saying we're here and to call us. We could leave the car here and walk to the mall and have coffee."

Diana agreed. She wanted to get to the bottom of the matter of the Trust Fund as soon as possible, but it would be nice to have some sister time with Celeste. The girls walked to the mall filled with cafés, myriad boutiques, restaurants, and tempting bookstores.

"What do you want to do first?" Celeste asked. "Coffee, or could I just pop into the art shop first? I wanted to check out their art supplies."

"Sure," Diana said but just then her cell phone rang. She checked the screen. "It's Aunt Evangeline." Diana listened for a moment then said, "We'll tell you when we see you. Is it okay to come straight back? Okay, see you soon."

"Murphy's Law," Celeste groaned. "As soon as

we get here, we have to go back. Typical."

Diana patted her on the shoulder. "Never mind, we'll come back one day soon."

Aunt Evangeline was waiting. She immediately ushered Diana and Celeste into the house and handed each girl a refreshing soda. Aunt Evangeline led the girls through the house to the pool which was at the back of the house.

"Aunt Evangeline, do you mind if we ask you a question?"

"Of course not, Diana. I'm intrigued. Sit down first. Sorry I missed you. I was at golf." Aunt Evangeline gestured to the deck chairs under shady umbrellas, sitting behind the pool.

"Aunt Evangeline, I'll come straight to the point. Is there a Trust Fund for Allegra, Celeste, and me?"

Aunt Evangeline's face changed expression at once. "What do you mean?"

"Aunt Evangeline, please tell us. Is there a Trust Fund?"

"That's something you should ask your father, Diana." Aunt Evangeline's tone was kindly but firm.

"I did."

"Oh." Aunt Evangeline seemed surprised. "What did he say?"

"He got angry and refused to answer, and I didn't want to push it, given his condition."

Aunt Evangeline shook her head. "It's not my place to say anything if your father won't, dear."

"Aunt Evangeline, please. Please!"

Celeste weighed in. "Aunt Evangeline, if you won't tell us, at least tell us who Mom's lawyer was. If there's a Trust Fund, we'd like to know about it."

"Do you need money, girls? If so, you could've

always come to me. There's no need to be embarrassed."

"Aunt Evangeline, it's not about the money." Diana was exasperated. "We just want to know whether there's a Trust Fund, or not. If you won't tell us, at least tell us who the lawyer is."

"The lawyer?"

"The lawyer who is the trustee of the Trust Fund." Diana said each word loudly and clearly.

Aunt Evangeline looked puzzled, and then laughed. "Are you trying to trick me?" she asked, and then laughed again. "I *will* tell you, but your father will be very angry with me if he finds out, so don't be in a hurry to tell him I've told you."

Both girls nodded.

"Yes, there is a Trust Fund, and each of you will come into it at the age of thirty. I know that's five to nine or so years later than most Trust Funds, but I had nothing to do with it, so don't blame me."

Diana and Celeste exchanged glances. "Is it worth much?" Celeste asked.

"I don't know the details, but with Trust Funds, there are fees taken out all the time, and those eat into the fund. There are quite a few expenses."

"I didn't know that." It was Celeste who spoke. Diana was still digesting the fact that she, Celeste, and Allegra had a Trust Fund and that no one had breathed a word of it to the sisters all these years.

"Oh yes. The trustee has to meet with the probate court on a regular basis to show that the Trust is being handled responsibly and under the terms of the will. The longer someone has to wait for the Trust to be paid, the higher the fees. All the expenses and fees are deducted from the estate."

Diana and Celeste both nodded. "Does this mean that there isn't much left in the Trust now?" Celeste asked.

Aunt Evangeline shook her head. "On the contrary, the Trust Fund will make you all wealthy women."

Diana looked at Celeste, who seemed dazed, taking it all in. "Constantine," she said softly.

Celeste nodded. "Scoundrel!"

Aunt Evangeline was visibly shocked. "What do you mean? Do you mean Constantine Connors? What does he have to do with anything? What has he done?"

"I know you were doing your matchmaking thing, Aunt Evangeline, but he wanted to date both me and Celeste, and we suspect he did it for our money. He would know about the Trust Fund, being Dad's lawyer."

"Oh no, you have it all wrong, Diana. Constantine's a *lovely* man," Evangeline protested. "He has his own money. You have it all wrong. You're both very attractive young ladies. Of course, he's attracted to you! That's all there is to it. He's a charming man."

Celeste shook her head at Diana as if to say, "Don't bother. She won't believe us."

Diana nodded back. Aunt Evangeline did not appear to have noticed the interchange.

"Why wouldn't Dad tell us?" Diana asked.

Aunt Evangeline took off her sunglasses, reached over, and patted Diana on the knee. "Your father feels very badly about the Trust Fund. He and your mother argued over it. Ethan said there was no need for it, and said your mother's wanting to establish it showed she didn't trust him with money. And truth be told, she didn't. Well, you know how he is with money."

Both girls nodded.

Evangeline continued. "Ethan felt so bad

about it, and then when he did lose all his money and had to sell out to the Wittmers, I'm certain that he felt it was proof that he couldn't handle money and had nothing to leave you. He must be very embarrassed."

"He'll have to tell us sooner or later, Aunt Evangeline. Diana will be thirty soon."

"I know, Celeste, but he'll probably want to keep his head in the sand a bit longer. And you girls should let him, given his heart condition and all."

"Do you know who the trustee lawyer is, Aunt Evangeline?" Diana asked.

"No idea, girls, sorry. Only your father would know. Your mother did tell me, but I can't remember. It was too long ago."

On the way home, Celeste called Allegra to share the news. Diana was distraught that she had taken Aunt Evangeline's counsel ten years earlier. She had looked up to Evangeline and thought her very wise, and Evangeline had persuaded her to break off her relationship with Jethro, and had even encouraged her to go to New York. Aunt Evangeline had all but vilified Jethro, but now was extolling the virtues of Constantine Connors, a man whose character Diana knew to be suspect, at the very least, and who had sent her friend Abigail bankrupt.

Diana remembered the verse in James chapter one verse five, which says we can ask God for wisdom and He will give it to us liberally. *I should have asked Him for wisdom ten years ago*, she thought bitterly. With Celeste chattering away on the phone to a most surprised Allegra, Diana sent up a silent prayer to God.

CHAPTER THIRTEEN

Diana's protests had fallen on deaf ears. Celeste insisted the two of them help Mrs. Yoder, an elderly Amish lady recently widowed.

"But there are plenty of Amish people who will help her," Diana protested. *Besides, I don't want to see Jethro*, she silently added.

Celeste waved one finger at her. "Dad insists. He's grateful to the Wittmer family and he wants to show that we will help their neighbors."

Diana raised her eyebrows. "He doesn't *act* grateful!"

Celeste shook her head. "Nevertheless, he *is* grateful. Anyway, I told Mrs. Wittmer that we'd help her, and we can't refuse."

Diana wiped one hand over her eyes. "I suppose you're right." She gestured to a bowl of apples on the countertop. "I was going to bake an apple pie."

"You can bake an apple pie at Mrs. Yoder's," Celeste said cheerily as she took Diana by the arm.

When Celeste stopped the car outside a white farmhouse, Diana cast her eyes around for Jethro. She didn't see him, but two Amish buggies were there. All Amish buggies looked alike to Diana and the horses weren't hitched to the buggies. She assumed the horses were in the stalls.

What would she do if Jethro was there?

Diana followed Celeste up the stairs to the front door past the old Adirondack chair with a fat tabby cat sitting next to it. Diana bent down to stroke the cat but she ran away.

Before anyone could knock, the door opened. Diana expected to see an elderly Amish lady standing there, but to her surprise it was Lavender.

"Lavender!" she exclaimed, followed quickly by, "It's nice to see you."

Lavender looked at her absently. "*Wilkom*."

Diana wondered why Lavender spoke in Pennsylvania Dutch. Was it simply because she was in an Amish house? Or was she going to become Amish?

"Come and meet Mrs. Yoder," Lavender said. She led them into the living room which was furnished like most Amish homes—minimalist, with no wall decoration. An old wooden Ansonia clock sat upon a chest in the corner. The tabby cat ran through Diana's legs and jumped onto the knee of the lady sitting on the couch, knitting.

"Hello, Mrs. Yoder," Diana said. "I'm Diana Hunt."

The lady waved a hand at her. "*Nee*, call me Betty. And this is Butter."

Diana smiled. "Butter?"

"As a kitten, she would jump on the countertop to find butter," Mrs. Yoder said with a laugh. "*Denki* for helping me today."

Two little girls walked into the room. Sarah ran over and flung her arms around Diana.

"*Hiya*, Sarah and Rose," Diana said. "I didn't know you'd be here today."

"We're baking," Rose said. "*Datt's* outside with our *onkel* mending fences. Are you going to help us bake, *Aenti* Diana?"

Diana plastered a broad smile on her face. "I sure am! What are we baking first?"

Sarah took her by the hand and led her into the kitchen.

"We're making pot pie," Lavender said. She gestured to the pastry strips hanging over the back of the chairs. "Sarah and Rose have been a great help laying out the pastry. We'll cut it as soon as it's dry."

"Yes, I can see the pastry looks just right. *Wunderbar*," Diana said with a smile.

"What can we do to help?" Celeste asked.

Lavender gestured to a large basket of apples sitting on the bench next to what was obviously fresh mint, judging by the scent. "Could you make an apple pie?"

Celeste chuckled. "I told you you'd get your wish."

Lavender looked puzzled. Diana said, "Sure. I'll get to it right away."

"Can I help you?" Sarah asked.

"Yes, you can help me peel the apples." Diana handed one to Sarah and was surprised how quickly the little girl peeled the apple. "We'll have this pie baked in no time," she said with a smile.

Diana had only peeled about five or so apples when Lavender spoke to her. "Do you mind if I ask you something?"

Diana's breath caught in her throat. "Sure," she said, although she was a little concerned.

"You nearly became Amish once."

Diana nodded. She hoped Lavender wouldn't bring up the fact that she was once engaged to Jethro, not with his daughters in the room.

"Obviously, it would have been a difficult decision." Diana nodded again. Lavender pushed on. "What, so what problems did you see ahead of you?"

Diana shrugged one shoulder. "The difficult ones, of course. It's an entirely different culture. I had to decide whether or not I could accept that."

Lavender appeared interested. "What, specifically?"

Lavender looked at Rose and Sarah, but they did not appear to be listening. "The practicalities, such as no electricity…"

Lavender interrupted her. "Some people live without electricity. Plenty of *Englischers* live off the grid."

"Sure," Diana said, "but I'm used to the Internet. And television. I watch television to relax."

"You could read instead," Lavender offered.

Diana nodded. "True. Still, being Amish is not

just about living off the grid and having the clothing rules. It's not just about not driving a car. The pace of life is much slower..."

Once more, Lavender interrupted her. "But surely more satisfying in many ways?"

Diana stared at Lavender. Was Lavender indeed thinking of becoming Amish? She wondered if she could be so bold as to ask her, and so framed her question carefully. "Does the Amish way of life hold attractions for you, Lavender?"

To her surprise, Lavender's face turned beet red. "Um, err, yes, it could in some ways," she stammered. It took her a moment to recover. "Do you think it's possible for an *Englischer* to become Amish?"

"Yes, I've heard of people who have done it, but not many have."

Lavender nodded. "There's a lady in a nearby community who became Amish about twelve years ago. My grandmother knows her. Would you visit her with me?"

"Sure," Diana said before she had a chance to think. "But why?"

Lavender looked up from rolling pastry. "Um, I don't know. I just thought it might be interesting. I mean, I'm interested in the subject of *Englischers* becoming Amish, to be honest."

Diana's stomach sank. It was becoming more apparent by the minute that Lavender was considering becoming Amish. Maybe, she was interested in Jethro, after all. And maybe it was mutual.

When the apple pie was in the oven to bake, Lavender said, "Let's all take a break. I'll make the meadow tea and we can bring out these whoopie pies."

"I'll take them. How's your foot?"

"Much better thanks. It doesn't hurt at all now."

Diana placed plates of whoopie pies in the living room.

Betty looked up from her knitting. "*Denki* for this. My hands are arthritic. That's why I'm knitting, as the *doktor* said I should keep using them. Honor Hershberger gave me some herbs for it, and they do help."

Diana was about to say something, when Lavender said, "I'll go and get the men."

"Too late," Betty said with a laugh. "Rose has already gone to fetch Jethro."

Seconds later, Jethro walked through the door, accompanied by Ezra.

Diana noticed that Lavender's face had turned beet red again.

Jethro appeared shocked to see Diana. "Diana! I didn't know you'd be here." He quickly added, "It's *gut* of you to help. *Hiya*, Celeste, Lavender."

"I said we would help the other day," Celeste said. "Where's Jeremiah?"

"He's working today," Jethro said.

Ezra chuckled. "He's doing our jobs as well as his own today."

Betty waved at them. "Come inside and have some whoopie pies that these lovely women baked." The cat, Butter, jumped from her lap and ran from the room into the kitchen. Diana hoped she hadn't left any butter on the countertop.

Diana was most uncomfortable sitting there making small talk with the others. Thankfully, the talk soon turned to construction, so she didn't have to join in the conversation.

Celeste seemed most interested in talking about barns. "So, are you doing many barn renovations at the moment?"

"We are working on several, but there's one main one we're focusing on at the moment," Ezra said. "These days, most *Englischers* want the floor strengthened in bank barns so they can drive their trucks in."

Diana was interested, in spite of being uncomfortable in Jethro's presence. "Do you build new barns or is it all barn repair now?"

"We do build some new barns and they're anything from steel to mortise and tenon construction," Jethro said. Their eyes locked, and something passed between them—or was it just Diana's imagination? She couldn't be sure. She risked a glance at Lavender and saw her staring at the brothers.

Something was definitely going on with Lavender—but what?

CHAPTER FOURTEEN

Diana was still unsure why she had agreed to visit with Mary Zook. She had a fairly good notion of what it was like to be Amish—after all, she had *almost* become Amish ten years earlier. Maybe, Lavender didn't realize Diana still had feelings for Jethro and saw Diana as an ally.

Mary Zook lived on a farm. By the crops and apple trees on the way to the farmhouse, Diana figured Mary's family's business was apple orchards, tomatoes, bean, and potatoes. She was a little nervous about meeting the woman.

When Lavender stopped the car and Diana got out, she saw an Amish woman in the herb garden. The woman stood up and waved.

"That's Mary Zook," Lavender told her.

Mary bustled over to them. "Oh, it's lovely to see you, Lavender."

Lavender wasted no time introducing Diana.

The two women smiled at each other. "Lavender tells me you nearly became Amish ten years ago," Mary blurted out.

Diana gasped. "Oh, um, yes," she stuttered.

Mary frowned deeply. "I hope I haven't said the wrong thing?"

Diana bit her lip. "I'm a bit embarrassed about it, to be honest. I broke the engagement with no warning and then immediately went to New York."

Mary shot her a shrewd look. "Kannscht du Pennsilfaanisch Deitsch schwetzer?" *Can you speak Pennsylvania Dutch?*

Diana nodded. "*Jah*."

Mary popped the thyme leaves she had just picked in her basket. "And do you ever regret your decision?"

Diana thought over her answer. She noticed Lavender was staring at her fixedly. "Well, yes," she said in the most nonchalant tone she could muster. "I do, from time to time."

"Please come inside and share lunch with me. I'm looking forward to chatting with both of you."

Diana was relieved to see Lavender was still smiling. Maybe, she hadn't taken Diana's words to heart, or maybe she wasn't threatened that Diana had admitted regretting her decision.

The Amish house looked the same as the houses in Jethro's community—no decoration and fairly sparse. Two hickory rockers sat side by side on the wooden floor, each with a round brown mat under them. Opposite the chairs stood two sturdy couches at an angle. Dark blue curtains hung on the windows behind a large kerosene lamp.

Mary ushered them into the kitchen. The kitchen had ample countertop space, and plenty of preserving bottles. An old oak table sat in the middle of the room. A single dark curtain was pulled to the side at the kitchen window.

Diana crossed to look out. The view was over the barn to the rolling hills beyond. Diana sighed. A similar view would have been hers if she had married Jethro. She rubbed her eyes and then realized her action would have caused streaks of mascara to run down her face. She chuckled. *This wouldn't have happened if I was Amish*, she thought.

Mary handing her a dish of creamed corn broke Diana from her reverie. She followed Mary and Lavender out to the dining table. They deposited plates of mashed potatoes, bacon and eggs, and thick slices of bread on the table.

Diana's nervousness had not abated. Mary was clearly someone who spoke her mind. She hoped Mary wouldn't ask her difficult questions about her relationship with Jethro, especially not in front of Lavender.

After they bowed their heads for the silent prayer, Mary came straight to the point. "So, you have come here today to ask me about my experience of becoming Amish?"

Both women nodded.

Mary looked up at the ceiling. "Not many

Englischers become Amish as I'm sure you're aware. Lavender, I know your *grossmammi* joined the community, but she had been Amish to start with. It's a simple life with a slow pace, but the thing I found the most difficult..."

She would have said more, but Lavender interrupted her. "What was the most difficult thing you found about becoming Amish? Was it the lack of electricity?"

Mary chuckled. "No, it was the rules. I know many Christian denominations in the English world do have strict rules, but I wasn't raised in one of those, so I found it more difficult. Still, once I realized the rules were not unreasonable. I had no trouble following them."

"What sort of rules exactly?" Lavender asked.

Mary set down her fork. "Well, everything really. Like how you have to do what the bishop says, but he is a kindly man who doesn't say anything too difficult to follow. Of course, there are the rules such as no electricity, no phones, no mirrors, having to wear the same type of clothes, not cutting the hair, having to wear the bonnets and all that. It took a bit of getting used to since I wasn't born into it, but now I wouldn't be able to go back to my old way of life."

Diana was interested in the conversation and what Mary had to say. "And you've never regretted this way of life?"

Mary chuckled. "I wouldn't say I've never regretted it. But I can honestly say I couldn't go back to being English. This is my life now."

"Did it take you long to adjust?" Lavender asked her.

Mary swallowed a mouthful of creamed celery before answering. "I was raised on a farm so I was used to hard work. I knew how to bake and make my own clothes, so it wasn't all that different. It would be hard for an *Englischer* who came from a city to take up the quietness of the country, but it wasn't an extra burden for me." She looked pointedly at Diana as she spoke.

Diana shifted on her seat. Did Mary think Diana was contemplating becoming Amish again?

"I think you're either a country person or a city person," Mary continued. "If you're a city person at heart, then you will find it much harder to get used to the quietness and the slow pace of life. Still, I'm sure there would be some city people who would love to live a quiet life and wouldn't find it boring."

Lavender helped herself to some more mashed potatoes before speaking. "And do you ever get bored?"

Mary burst into laughter. When she had sufficiently recovered, she said, "*Nee!* I have five *kinner* between the ages of four and ten. Who can be bored with so many children? I work from dawn to dusk, so there's no time to get bored."

Diana looked around the room. "Where are they now?"

"The four-year-old is helping his father, and the others are at school," Mary said.

"Your husband didn't come in for lunch today?" Diana asked in the hopes that her presence hadn't scared them away.

"We're having an early lunch. They'll come in for a later lunch," Mary said. "The farrier is here shoeing the horses and won't be finished for another hour or two."

"And did you find it hard to learn to drive a buggy?" Lavender asked her.

Mary seemed to think her question was particularly funny. "*Nee*, like I said, I was raised on a farm. I'm used to horses. Of course, I used to ride them and not drive them, but it was easy to learn to drive. I can't say it wasn't frustrating at first, not being able to drive a car and so everything takes so much longer, and at first I missed Facebook and Instagram, but we do have a phone in the barn because of the business. If I'd had to drive the buggy to the shanty every time I needed to make a call, I would have found that quite difficult."

Diana and Lavender nodded.

Mary slathered a thick layer of butter on her bread. "And many people find learning the language difficult. You can't join the community without being fluent in Pennsylvania Dutch. You know, becoming Amish isn't just about speaking the language or the lack of technology," she said. "It's a strong community. No one is on their own. If something goes wrong, the whole community rallies around to help. For example, the Addleman *familye's* barn was struck by lightning the other week and the community has already raised a new barn for them. I value the strong sense of community. And, of course, faith is paramount to our lives as Amish."

"What beliefs do you have that are different?" Lavender asked her.

Mary shrugged. "Many Christian denominations have different beliefs," she said. "Catholics and Protestants have different beliefs, of course. Amish are Anabaptists, so we believe in adult baptism. We believe in hard work. We also believe that God has appointed one woman for every man. We believe that whatever happens is God's will. We are a peaceful people. That's why we avoid legal matters, and so on. Are there any other questions you'd like to ask?"

Lavender spoke up. "Are there any theological differences?"

Mary looked down at her hands for a few minutes before speaking. "Some other Christian groups also believe in adult baptism

—but as for differences? You probably know that many communities don't approve of quoting Scripture as they consider it prideful, but I will quote a Scripture, Romans 12:2, because to me it sums up precisely why the Amish are different.

> 'And be not conformed
> to this world: but be
> ye transformed by
> the renewing of your
> mind, that ye may
> prove what is that
> good, and acceptable,
> and perfect, will of
> God.'"

She added, "So having buggies and having no electricity and our clothing and so on ensures that we are not conformed to this world. Does that make sense?"

Diana and Lavender exchanged glances. "Yes,

you've been very helpful," Lavender said. "I thought you'd say that no one should ever become Amish." She broke off and laughed.

"I most certainly wouldn't advise anyone to do it lightly," Mary said. "People raised English are used to a fast pace of life, an entirely different way of life. Even a most devout Christian could find being Amish difficult to a degree. Someone who's been raised one way will always find it difficult to move into an entirely different culture. It's a culture shock."

She cleared her throat and then added, "Sometimes, we are too consumed with the things that we want, to see the things that we have."

"If you don't mind me asking, did you become Amish because you met your husband and fell in love with him?" Lavender asked her.

Mary appeared to be pondering the question. "It would never have occurred to me to become Amish if I hadn't met Levi. Levi and I couldn't be together unless we were both English or both Amish, and it was obvious Levi was never going to be English. So, if I wanted to marry him, I had to become Amish. Are you still hungry? How about some Schnitz pie?"

"That would be lovely," Diana said as she made to stand.

Mary waved her back down. "*Nee*, stay there. It won't take me long to fetch it. It's only one pie." She chuckled.

Mary soon returned to the table with a huge apple pie. After she cut it into slices, she added, "You hear people say no one should become Amish for a man, but there's more to it than that. Obviously, if I hadn't met Levi and fallen in love, then I would never have become Amish. He was the catalyst, but it was a big decision. I had to think and pray on it at some length and then I spoke with the bishop —also at length."

"And the bishop didn't try to discourage you?" Lavender asked her.

Mary shook her head. "As I said earlier, we Amish believe that there is one woman for every man and one man for every woman. I think that's why the bishop didn't discourage me, but he and his wife both explained to me what it was like to become Amish. Still, it's one thing to hear it."

Lavender nodded slowly. "Yes, the theory would be one thing, but it would be another thing to practice it."

Mary readily agreed. "If somebody was thinking of becoming Amish, I would caution them to think it through long and hard." She broke off and chuckled again. "That sounded obvious. Of course, anybody *would* think about it long and hard. I suppose I'm trying to say that if you are considering becoming Amish, then picture how you would be, going about your daily life, no make-up, no fashionable clothes, but working hard with your hands and driving a buggy everywhere. Somewhere that would take you half an hour in a car would take you a few hours to drive your horse at a trot."

She nodded slowly. "I suppose it would be like going back in time. Of course, there's the wonderful sense of community and living a life of faith, but on the other hand, family members would no doubt think somebody who became Amish was quite mad. Not many of us have done it," she added. "And you would need to find a community that was open to seekers. Some communities are not."

"What's a seeker?" Diana asked.

"Someone who wants to join the Amish."

After she stopped speaking, the three women ate their Schnitz pie in silence.

Diana had already contemplated becoming Amish ten years earlier and had thought she would be able to do it, but had suddenly decided against it with Aunt Evangeline's words in her ear constantly. Still, she couldn't blame her aunt—she was the one who had made the decision.

Could she, in fact, join the Amish community after living a fast-paced life in New York?

CHAPTER FIFTEEN

"I've often thought about becoming Amish," Celeste announced over breakfast.

Diana gave a little start, spilling coffee on the kitchen table. She jumped up to find something to clean it.

"Surely, it couldn't have been that much of a shock," Celeste said with a chuckle.

Diana cleaned up the spilled coffee before answering. "It *is* a big shock. I thought I was the only person I knew who had thought about becoming Amish."

"Apart from Lavender," Celeste said pointedly, before adding, "Why not?"

Diana tapped Celeste's perfectly manicured fingernails before sitting down. "You're always having manicures and pedicures. I can't imagine your fingernails with dirt under them."

Celeste looked offended. "Just how superficial do you think I am, Diana?"

"Um, her, it's not that I think you're superficial," Diana began, but Celeste interrupted her.

"I'm not superficial at all! Of course, I want to look my best, but if I were an Amish person, I wouldn't so much care. Well, I'd still watch my figure, but I'd be quite happy not to wear make-up."

"You have flawless skin," Diana pointed out.

Celeste frowned deeply. "That's not the point. You know, I think I could easily become Amish."

Diana disagreed. "I don't think anybody becomes Amish *easily*," she said.

Celeste stood up. "Honestly, Diana. You seem quite irritable this morning." Diana opened her mouth to protest, but Celeste pushed on. "You were once thinking about becoming Amish, so why can't I think about it?"

Diana sighed. "No, of course, you can think about it. So, are you actually considering it?"

Celeste shrugged one shoulder. "I'm not actually considering it at this point, but I don't think I'd have as much difficulty as you think. I *do* like the simple life. After all, I didn't move to New York like you did." She held up one hand, palm outward. "I wasn't being mean by that remark. I just meant that I'm happy with the simple life."

"But could you live without electricity, phone, Internet, and Netflix?" Diana asked, keeping her tone even so as not to offend Celeste any further.

Celeste looked off into the distance. "Yes, I've given it some thought and I think I could, but only if I had a good reason. That is, if I fell in love with an Amish man."

Diana could not resist asking. "Like Jeremiah?"

"Jeremiah?" Celeste's eyes shot skyward. "Why would you mention Jeremiah? He's just a close friend. In fact, I'm trying to think of some Amish ladies I can match him up with. He shouldn't be single at his age."

Diana was about to respond when a knock on the door forestalled her. "I'll get it," Celeste said. "You finish your coffee."

Diana assumed it was Lori at the door, so she was shocked when Jethro and his daughters, Rose and Sarah, came into the kitchen.

Sarah hurried over and scrambled into Diana's lap. She gave Diana a big hug, which Diana returned.

"Diana, I've come to ask you a favor," Jethro said.

Diana's heart skipped a beat. "A favor?" she parroted. "Um, sure."

Jethro tipped his head. "In private?"

Diana was aware her jaw had fallen open. What possible favor could Jethro possibly ask her?

"Okay, we can step outside," Diana said.

"I'll mind the girls," Celeste said.

Diana stepped through the kitchen door into the fresh air and walked over to a stately old beech tree under which were bladdernut bushes dripping with beautiful lily-of-the-valley-like flowers. The heavenly scent of vanilla custard floated through the air. She came straight to the point. "Jethro, what did you want to ask me?"

Jethro's face flushed. "I hope it's not too much of an imposition, but the Amish knitting circle ladies have asked my *dochders* to attend. Rose has been by herself, but I'd like Sarah to go too. After all, she's past the age to start to learn knitting."

Diana held back a smile. Only the Amish would think a four-year-old child was past the age to start to learn a skill. Aloud she said, "How can I be of help?"

"Would you take Sarah and Rose to the knitting circle?"

"But I'm English," Diana said. "Would the Amish ladies mind?"

"Of course not," Jethro said. "They'd be happy to see you. In fact, I asked Susanna Glick if she would mind. I also told her I hadn't spoken with you about it yet. Please don't feel obliged."

Diana's heart was beating out of her chest. Jethro had asked her to take his daughters to a knitting circle. Why hadn't he asked Lavender to take them? The possibilities ran through her mind. Could it be because he didn't want the Amish ladies to suspect about him and Lavender?

Jethro was still speaking. "They don't have a *mudder*, and there is nobody to take them."

How could Diana refuse after he said something like that? "Yes, I'd be happy to take them," she said, a thousand butterflies fluttering around her stomach at Jethro's proximity.

"*Wunderbar!*" he said. "*Denki*, Diana." Still, the wariness did not leave his face.

Her heart melted at the way he said her name. "When is it?"

"Today, soon," he said. "Do you have other plans?"

Diana shook her head. "No, that's fine."

"I have one more favor to ask," said Jeremiah. "Would you drive them there in the buggy rather than in your car?"

Diana was puzzled and she said so. "Why is that important?"

"It's important to me because..." His words trailed away and he seemed to be searching for the right words. Finally, he said, "It would just make things more normal for my *dochders*."

Diana nodded slowly. "Sure."

"Do you still remember how to drive a buggy?"

Diana nodded. He pushed on. "Then why don't we drive to my *haus* now and then you can take the buggy on to Susanna Glick's *haus*. Rose knows the way."

"Sure."

Before long, Diana was back in Jeremiah's buggy, just like she had been ten years earlier. Rose talked excitedly in the back seat while Sarah clutched her doll, and Diana thought about how things might have been. To her it seemed to be the same buggy—only the horse was different. If she had married Jeremiah ten years earlier, then she would be in the buggy just like this. The weight of Diana's mistake lay heavily upon her.

Mrs. Wittmer was tending to the garden when Jeremiah drove up. He jumped out and handed the reins to Diana. As their hands touched lightly, electric jolts ran through Diana's body. She schooled her features into neutral, hoping Jethro hadn't seen her reaction.

Mrs. Wittmer waved to her, a big smile

plastered on her face. *She must've known about this*, Diana thought.

"So, you're confident with the buggy?" Jeremiah said. "This horse is sensible. Rose even drives him on occasion."

"I'll be fine," Diana said. She turned the horse around and then clicked her on into a steady trot.

"I didn't know you could drive a buggy," Rose piped up. "Do you know the way to Mrs. Glick's *haus?*"

"Your father told me she lives in Saxony Lane Road," Diana said. "But I haven't been there before, so I'm hoping you girls can tell me the way."

"Of course, I can tell you the way," Rose said. "Sarah doesn't know the way because she's never been."

"I *do* know the way," Sarah said in a small

voice. "I've been in the buggy when *Datt's* taken you there."

As the girls argued, albeit gently, Diana smiled to herself. She was pleased to hear Sarah speak.

"And we have our knitting with us," Rose continued. "We're going to knit scarves."

"Scarves will be most useful in winter," Diana said, amused. "Oh, I just realized I haven't brought any wool or knitting needles."

"Mrs. Glick might have some spare ones for you," Rose said. "Maybe, after we knit a scarf for ourselves and one for *Datt*, we could knit a scarf for you."

"*Denki*," Diana said. "I would very much like that." She wondered if they would, in fact, be knitting a scarf for Lavender. She wondered how well they knew Lavender. She was unable to stop the wave of jealousy that flooded her at the thought of Lavender and Jethro together. Would they indeed get married? Her heart ached.

"Turn here," Rose called out. "It's the house at the end of this road. You can't go any further."

"*Denki* for guiding me," Diana said. "That was very helpful of you."

When she reached the house, she saw ladies standing out the front. It seemed the ladies had just arrived as they were hitching their horses to posts. She pulled alongside them. Rose jumped out first and tied up the horse before going back to help Sarah out of the buggy.

Diana regarded the Amish ladies shyly, but they greeted her with welcoming smiles. "*Hiya*, you must be Diana. Jethro was hoping you could bring his *dochders*. I'm Susanna Glick. This is Irma Schrock and this is Rhoda Peachey."

They all greeted each other. "I'm afraid I

didn't bring any wool or knitting needles," Diana said.

"I have plenty to spare," said Susanna. "The main thing is you've brought the girls."

Rose handed her a basket of whoopie pies.

"*Denki*, Rose," Susanna said. "All come inside. Let's have some garden tea and something to eat before we start our knitting."

Sarah hurried over to Diana and took her hand and then stood partially behind her.

Diana was already growing to love the little girls. Now her heart had more than one reason to break if Jethro married Lavender.

CHAPTER SIXTEEN

"The children seem taken with you," Irma said.

Diana simply smiled in reply. Sarah had pulled her chair close to Diana and had been clinging to her hand the whole time they had been drinking garden tea and eating whoopie pies, tapioca pudding, as well as pureed apples known as *Lattwaerig* spread thickly on bread.

Irma leaned forward and addressed Sarah. "We'll have to clean our hands and then we'll start knitting."

Sarah ducked her head behind Diana.

"Have you knitted much before, Diana?" Susanna asked her.

"Yes, quite a lot, but not lately," Diana admitted. "I used to enjoy knitting and crochet, and even tatting."

"Why don't you help Sarah? Rose, have you been knitting at home?"

Rose produced her knitting and showed Susanna.

Susanna nodded. "You *have* done quite a lot of knitting since last week. Come and sit by me and I'll help you." She turned to Diana and handed her some wool and a pair of knitting needles. "We're knitting scarves today because of the *kinner*, but feel free to make anything you wish."

Diana thanked her and then turned her attention to Sarah. "I'll cast on for you and then show you how to do it. What do you think of that?"

Sarah nodded shyly.

"Did you bring any knitting needles with you?"

Sarah handed knitting needles to Diana. Susanna looked over her shoulder and made a clicking sound with her tongue. "*Menner*! They have no idea about knitting. Those needles are far too thin for a beginner. I have just the knitting needles for you, Sarah. Come with me."

Sarah held out her hand to Diana who took her hand and followed Susanna to a storage room. Susanna pulled out a box and produced a pair of thick needles. "Would you like to use these, Sarah?"

Sarah looked at Diana, who quickly nodded. Sarah nodded and smiled before taking the knitting needles. "*Denki*, Mrs. Glick."

Susanna looked shocked, so Diana assumed that she hadn't heard the child speak for some time.

After Diana cast on, she demonstrated how to knit.

It didn't take Sarah long to catch on. Diana sat there the whole time wondering whether she should praise Sarah for her efforts, but knowing Amish don't like to praise in some circumstances. She was at a loss.

Susanna must have noticed her predicament, because she came over. "*Wunderbar*!" she exclaimed. "You have made *gut* progress, Sarah."

"*Denki*," said Sarah.

When Sarah was on her fifth row, with considerable help from Diana, Diana cast on her own scarf. The wool was dark blue. Her first instinct was to make a scarf for Jethro, but then her spirits fell. Lavender would be the one to make a scarf for Jethro. A wave of sadness hit her suddenly and she wiped a tear from her eye. She looked up to see Susanna looking at her, but Susanna quickly looked away.

Rose had been chatting to Irma the whole time. Diana bit back a smile. Irma certainly was good-natured. Diana loved the way the Amish cared for children. She had noticed that Amish children always had plenty of attention, and they thrived on it. To the Amish, every person was important. She loved the sense of community she was feeling at the knitting circle. Even though she was English, she felt included and safe. She had never felt that way in New York. Once more, she regretted her decision.

The women knitted for about an hour. Rose had not drawn breath the whole time.

"Let's have lunch," Susanna said. "Sarah and

Rose, why don't you help me? Do you both like wet bottom Shoo-fly pie?"

Sarah nodded, while Rose said, "Oh yes, I like it much better than dry bottom Shoo-fly pie. I think it's because it has more molasses. In fact, I don't like crusts or pastry on anything. With apple pies, I only like the apple and I don't like to eat the pie crust, but *Datt* says I have to eat the crust."

The girls followed Susanna into the kitchen with Rose still talking.

Irma burst into laughter. "I've never heard a child talk so much. It's a wonder I managed to concentrate on my knitting, although I did drop a few stitches." She held up the scarf for everyone to inspect.

"Dropping stitches keeps us humble," Rhoda said with a smile. "Did I hear Sarah speaking to Susanna earlier?"

"It was only a few words," Diana said.

"That's a few more words than she's spoken since her mother went to be with *Gott*," Rhoda said. "And Jethro didn't remarry."

"Yes, he's been burdened these last few years," Irma said. "Naomi is a big help with the *kinner*, but with all her *sohns* unmarried.... well, it's a lot of work for her to cook and wash for all the *menner* and care for the *kinner*. I'm sure she would be glad if Jethro found a *fraa*."

Both Irma and Rhoda looked pointedly at Diana.

"You were engaged to Jethro many years ago, weren't you," Rhoda said.

Before Diana could speak, Irma tapped Rhoda on the arm. "Hush, Rhoda. You're embarrassing her."

"That's all right," Diana said. "Yes, we were engaged. I was, um, young and foolish."

"You were young and foolish to get engaged to Jethro?" Rhoda asked.

Diana shook her head. "*Nee*, I was young and foolish to break the engagement."

Irma and Rhoda looked behind her. Diana swung around. Jethro was standing there at the door. She hadn't even heard the door open. Had Jethro heard what she said? And if so, what would he make of it?

She avoided his gaze but thankfully did not have to speak because Jethro's daughters ran out of the kitchen. "*Datt!*" they both squealed.

"You're early," Susanna said. "We were about to have lunch. Please join us."

Jethro looked as though he was about to object when Rose said, "Mrs. Glick has wet bottom Shoo-fly pie."

No doubt she would have said more, but Jethro asked, "And how was your knitting today?"

Both Rose and Sarah hurried over to fetch the knitting and both showed their father.

"You've made good progress today," Jethro said, admiring their handiwork.

"*Aenti* Diana helped me," Sarah said quietly.

"And Sarah spoke to me," Susanna said.

Jethro looked shocked, and then beamed from ear to ear. "*Wunderbar!*"

Susanna gestured to the big oak table. "Now, Sarah and Rose have set the table so please come and eat."

When they sat at the table, Sarah once more sat next to Diana and pulled her chair close to her. Diana saw that Jethro was carefully watching. When they opened their eyes after the silent prayer, Sarah noticed Jethro was staring at her. He quickly adverted his eyes.

Rose chatted throughout the lunch. Diana noticed Jethro was adept at changing the subject, much to her amusement. "We all knitted scarves today," Susanna told Jethro.

"I'm making a scarf for you," Rose told him.

"And who are you making a scarf for?" Susanna asked Sarah.

She pointed to herself, and everybody laughed.

"I told her to make a scarf for herself first and then to make a scarf for her father next," Diana explained. "Scarves for fathers are much bigger and it's always good to practice by making a scarf for oneself first."

Susanna nodded. "Very good advice."

Sarah looked at Susanna and beamed. Diana felt the child certainly was becoming braver with other people.

She noted Rose kept her eye on the wet bottom Shoo-fly pie and as soon as everyone had finished their meal of pot pie, Susanna gave Rose the first piece of Shoo-fly pie before serving the others.

Rose stared at Diana. "*Aenti* Diana, do you make Shoo-fly pie?"

Diana nodded. "As a matter of fact, I do. I make both dry bottom and wet bottom Shoo-fly pie, although like you, I do prefer the wet bottom Shoo-fly pie."

"And do you bake apple dumplings, funnel cakes, banana bread, poppy seed bread, and Long John rolls?" Rose asked her.

By now Diana was becoming uncomfortable. She wondered if Rose was sizing her up as a suitable match for her father. She thought the Amish ladies were thinking the same because they were exchanging glances and chuckling.

"*Jah*, I make all of those things," Diana said, keeping her tone light. Jethro shot her a long look, but she was unable to hold his gaze.

As soon as they had finished eating, Jethro stood up. "*Denki*, Susanna, for lunch and Irma and Rhoda as well for helping my *dochders*. We must be going."

"But you haven't had *kaffi*," Susanna protested.

"I have to get back to work," he said.

Diana thanked the ladies and made to follow Jethro out the door, but Susanna stopped her. "I hope you'll come every week. It's lovely to have you visit with us."

Diana didn't know what to say. She hadn't quit her job. It suddenly dawned on her. She had no intention of going back to New York. She wasn't sure when she had made the decision, but one thing was clear—she was never going back. She would have to put in a formal resignation. Nick would certainly be pleased.

"*Denki*, I'd like that," she said.

"Will you help me again?" Sarah asked.

"Of course, I will," Diana said. Sarah took Diana's hand and they walked to the buggy.

Diana lifted Sarah into the buggy while Jethro lifted in Rose.

As the horse trotted off, Jethro turned to Diana. "*Denki* for helping Sarah today, Diana," he said. "Don't feel obliged to keep doing it on a weekly basis."

Diana shot a glance into the back seat of the buggy. Sarah and Rose had their heads together, chatting away. "It was my pleasure," she said. "I had a lovely time."

Diana thought Jethro looked pleased, but was she mistaken? Was that his way of hinting that he didn't want her to continue at the knitting circle, that Lavender would soon be replacing her?

Jethro didn't say any more until he turned into the road leading up to the Whitley farm. "When are you going back to New York?" he asked.

"I'm not," she said. "I've decided to stay here."

Jethro smiled once more. This time, his delight was evident.

Why was he pleased she wasn't going back to New York? Was he looking for a babysitter so he could date Lavender? Yes, there was his mother, but Irma or Rhoda had said Naomi already was overloaded with caring for Rose and Sarah and with cooking for all her sons. Taking the girls to the knitting circle would certainly give Naomi more time and thus free up some time for Jethro to date Lavender.

Diana was expecting Jethro to drive her home, but he detoured into his own farm. "Where are you going?" she asked him.

"My mother has baked pies for you and your *familye*," he said. "She told me to collect them on the way to taking you home."

"That's very kind of her," Diana said.

When they reached the farm, Rose said, "Can we go with you to *Aenti* Diana's house, *Datt*?"

Jethro nodded. "*Jah*, you can come with me to *Aenti* Diana's house."

He hopped down from the buggy and said to Diana, "I'll go inside and get the pies from *Mamm*."

Just then, Jeremiah ran over. "There's a call for you in the barn."

Jeremiah looked surprised to see Diana. "*Hullo*, Diana. *Wie gehts?* How is Celeste?"

"I'm good, thanks, and so is Celeste," Diana said.

"I won't be long," Jethro said. He tied the horse to the rail and hurried to the barn.

Mrs. Wittmer opened the front door and waved to Diana. "*Hiya*, Diana. Where's Jethro?" She hurried down the stairs.

"He had to take a call in the barn," Diana said. "He'll be right back."

"How was your knitting?" Naomi asked the

girls.

They both held out their projects for her to inspect.

"That's a lot of knitting for one day," Naomi said, nodding slowly. "Diana, come inside and I'll fetch the bumbleberry pies I made for you and your family. Come inside," she said again.

Diana followed Naomi inside. She was concerned, as she had a feeling that Naomi wanted to say something to her. And it turned out she was right.

"I wanted to thank you for helping with Sarah," Naomi said. "She has certainly come out of her shell since you came back to town." Naomi narrowed her eyes. "When are you going back to New York?"

Diana shook her head. "I'm not going back."

Naomi looked relieved and pleased. "You can borrow the basket to keep the pies safe."

"Thank you so much," Diana said.

"It was kind of you to help Sarah with her knitting," Naomi said. "Jethro's been a lot happier lately."

Diana wondered what that remark meant, but she wasn't about to ask Naomi, and besides they were already back at the front door. Jethro was striding over to the buggy.

"I won't be long, *Mamm*," he said. "I'll take Diana home. The girls are coming with me."

"Take all the time you want," Naomi said with a smile at Diana.

As Jethro clicked the horse forward, a disquieting thought struck Diana. Did Naomi think she was the one who was going to marry Jethro? Naomi had certainly made some pointed remarks. Was Jethro keeping his relationship with Lavender a secret from his own mother?

CHAPTER SEVENTEEN

The following morning, Diana busied herself with writing a letter of resignation and organizing the cancelation of the lease on her apartment. She also called her boss to tell her in person. It was a most awkward conversation. Collette expressed surprise and wanted to know if she was going to another firm. It was clear that Collette didn't believe that Diana was staying in Lancaster and had no further plans to work as an advertising executive.

"And so, what exactly are your career plans?" Collette had asked her.

"I'm not quite sure at this point," she said honestly.

And what *were* her career plans? If anything, she would love to marry Jethro, but such plans were no good unless he felt the same way. And did he? At times it certainly seemed he did. But what about Lavender? Diana was entirely confused.

Celeste had been out shopping all morning and bounced into the living room where Diana was tapping away on her laptop. "What have you been doing?" she asked.

"I resigned," she said.

Celeste's mouth dropped open. "So, it is true that you're staying here?"

Diana did not have a chance to respond, as Celeste ran over and threw her arms around her neck. "Oh, I'm so excited! I've missed you. But what are you going to do?"

"Do?" Diana echoed.

"Do for a career?"

Diana chuckled. "That's what my boss asked me."

Celeste put her hands on her hips. "That's not an answer."

Diana waved one hand through the air. "I don't know, to be honest."

"Is it a man?"

"A man?"

Celeste sat down with a thud. "Honestly, Diana, stop repeating everything I say! What secrets are you keeping from me?"

"I'm not keeping any secrets, and don't speak too loudly because Dad's been a terrible mood all morning."

"He's been in *a lot* of terrible moods lately," Celeste said in lowered tones. "Anything in particular this time?"

"He didn't want the nurse to give him a blood test," Diana said.

Celeste pulled a face. "Who could blame him? Anyway, let's take some iced tea out to the front porch."

Diana stood up and stretched. "That sounds like a good idea."

The girls hadn't been sitting on the front porch for long when Celeste caught Diana's arm. "Look! There's a buggy heading this way."

"No doubt it's one of the Wittmers," Diana said. "Who else would it be?" She noticed Celeste's face lit up.

"It's not Jeremiah's horse," Celeste said after an interval.

The girls had to wait until the buggy arrived to see the occupants. Naomi jumped down from the buggy. Rose and Sarah waved to Diana from inside the buggy and she waved back.

"*Hiya*, Diana and Celeste. I have an emergency. Mary Swartzentruber is in labor and the midwives asked me to help her. She's two weeks early and it's her first baby. Would you mind looking after the girls for me?"

"We'd be happy to," Diana said. "Would Jethro mind?"

A look of confusion flashed across Naomi's face. "Why would he mind?" She shook her head. "*Nee*, he would be pleased that his daughters are experiencing some English ways. It will help them understand. I've left a note to Jethro to come and fetch them when he comes inside for lunch."

She helped the girls down from the buggy. Sarah, as usual, ran over and held Diana's hand tightly. "*Hiya, Aenti* Diana. *Hiya, Aenti* Celeste,*" Rose said, but Sarah hid behind Diana.

"*Denki,*" Naomi said before hopping in her buggy and driving back down the driveway at a fast trot.

Diana and Celeste exchanged glances. "Would you girls like some iced tea?" Celeste said.

Sarah nodded shyly, but Rose said, "*Jah, denki.* We love iced tea. *Mammi* doesn't make it much and we usually have hot meadow tea even in summer, but sometimes we have iced mint tea. It's nice, but sometimes *Mammi* doesn't put sugar in it and then it's not so nice."

By now, they were in the kitchen, and Celeste poured the girls some iced tea. "Now, what do we have to eat?" Celeste asked Diana with raised eyebrows.

"We still have some bumbleberry pie," Celeste said. "We can have it with ice cream."

Rose was at once on her feet. "Can I help?"

"Thank you for your kind offer, Rose, but you're a guest, so sit down and relax. Maybe you could help see that Sarah is all right," Diana said, doing her best to be tactful.

It seemed to do the trick because Rose moved her chair closer to Sarah and glanced at her from time to time.

"How do we entertain Amish kids?" Celeste whispered to Diana. "We can't show them TV or give them an iPad or anything."

"We could do some baking or some gardening," Diana whispered back. "Rose is particularly fond of wet bottom Shoo-fly pie, so we could make one."

Celeste drew her hand over her forehead. "That's a good idea. I must admit—I'm at a loss." She glanced at the children who were looking around the room, no doubt at the electrical appliances, with interest. "What did Mrs. Wittmer mean about it being good for them to become accustomed to the English?" she whispered.

Diana shrugged one shoulder. "Maybe because of Lavender."

Celeste nodded vigorously. "Yes, of course. That makes perfect sense. When Jethro and Lavender get married, the children will be visiting Lavender's English family on occasion." She nodded slowly as she spoke.

Rose, in particular, was thrilled to be making wet bottom Shoo-fly pie. Rose asked more questions about the sort of food Diana could cook and was thrilled to know that Diana was proficient with most Amish foods. "And do you make nice creamed celery?" she asked Diana.

"No one's complained about it so far, so it must be nice," Diana said with a chuckle.

Rose appeared to be thinking it over. "But they might have only been polite," she said. "*Datt* says if we don't like food, it's not polite to say so."

Diana laughed. "I'll make you some creamed celery one day and you can tell me if it's nice."

Rose nodded solemnly. "That's a *gut* idea."

"Have you made many Shoo-fly pies?" Celeste asked the girls.

As usual, Rose was the one who answered. "Not by myself, but Sarah and I help *Mammi*. Sometimes she makes dry bottom pies." Her nose wrinkled in distaste.

"Then how many pies do you think we should make?" Diana asked her.

"We could make two or maybe three," Rose said hopefully.

Diana leaned over the countertop. "I have an idea. Why don't we make one for you to take home and we'll make another one that we can eat now—unless your *vadder* comes back too soon, before we finish baking."

Rose looked alarmed at the thought. Diana set all-purpose flour, brown sugar, and shortening on the countertop. "Would you like to make the crumbs, Rose?"

Rose enthusiastically rubbed in the ingredients with her fingers to make fine crumbs, while Diana dissolved the baking soda in boiling water. "Sarah, could you help me stir in the molasses, corn syrup, egg and salt?" She watched Sarah carefully to make sure she would not come into contact with the hot liquid. However, Sarah was clearly already a capable baker.

When that was done, Diana poured one-third of the mixture into the unbaked pie crust and sprinkled one-third of the crumbs over this mixture. She repeated the process until all the ingredients were used up. "Now we have to bake it for forty minutes," she said.

Jethro's timing was good, because there was a knock on the door just as Diana was taking the pies from the oven. "I'll get it," Celeste said.

She returned presently with Jethro. Diana at once noticed his face was grim.

"Look, we made those Shoo-fly pies," Rose said with delight. "We're taking one home with us. Could we have some for lunch? We were going to have some now, but you've come too soon."

"Yes, we can have some for lunch," Jethro said in clipped tones. "It's very kind of you to look after Rose and Sarah. *Denki*, Diana and Celeste."

"I borrowed this basket from your mother so I'll put the Shoo-fly pie in it for you to take back to her," Diana said.

Jethro thanked her again. Celeste's phone rang, so Diana showed Jethro and the girls out of the house. Jethro helped the girls into the buggy and then walked back to Diana who was standing on the porch. "Diana, I'm sorry my mother burdened you with this."

"It wasn't a burden at all!" Diana explained. "I love spending time with your girls." *And with you*, she added silently.

Deep furrows lined Jethro's brow. "It might not be good for you to spend so much time with the girls. Maybe I shouldn't have asked you to take them to the knitting circle. They're getting too attached. Diana, I need to discuss something with you."

He would have said more, but they heard yelling inside the house. Celeste ran out. "Diana, please come. Dad's refusing to have his blood pressure taken. The poor nurse!"

Diana looked back at Jethro, but he was already half way to his buggy.

Whatever did he mean? Did he mean it wasn't good for his daughters to spend time with her when he was going to marry Lavender? Was he concerned they were more attached to her than they were to Lavender?

A tear rolled down her cheek.

CHAPTER EIGHTEEN

There was no sign of Jethro for the rest of the day, and Diana could not muster the courage to go to the Wittmer farm to ask him why he wanted to speak to her. Consequently, she paced up and down the house for what seemed like hours. Her stomach was churning and her heart was racing. Never had she been so tense.

Allegra had come over to discuss the Trust with her sisters, and both Allegra and Celeste put Diana's anxious behavior down to the news of the Trust Fund.

Diana tossed and turned all night, and through the night went to the kitchen three times for a glass of water. She arose at six, and kept pacing.

Breakfast tasted like cardboard, but Diana forced some down. She could imagine her stomach growling embarrassingly while talking to Jethro if she did not.

"Diana, why don't you go for a ride?"

Diana regarded Celeste with surprise. "But I don't own a horse!"

Celeste shrugged. "Jeremiah and Jethro said we can ride whenever we like, so long as we only ride Snow or Tammy," she said.

Diana thought it over. "Maybe a ride would be good for me." Diana dressed quickly and left the Stone House to walk down to the barn.

The path to the barn seemed to stretch on forever. Diana walked past the white Evening Primrose flowers, oblivious to their syrupy scent. She ignored the columbine and the trailing arbutus clustering around the blooms of the Mock Orange. She did not even notice the intense fragrance of the gorgeous lilac-pink flowers of the lilac shrubs. As she approached the barn, Diana did, however, notice the scent of hay, of horses, and of dust, a scent much loved by horse people but not usually enjoyed by others. To Diana, it was comforting and reassuring.

As Diana rounded the corner, Jethro was leading a pony out of the stall. The pony was saddled. "Diana!" Jethro looked surprised.

"Hi, Jethro." Diana had been so keen to speak to Jethro, but now she was dumbstruck.

"Would you like to go for a ride?"

When Diana did not answer, Jethro

continued. "You can ride Snow, and I'll ride Ash."

Diana did not know what to say. "I thought Amish didn't ride? I mean, I know the children do, but adults?" As soon as she spoke, she remembered he had told her that he rode horses he was training. How could she have forgotten?

"I'm making sure Ash is safe for my children. I'd asked Jeremiah to ride Snow with me, but he had to help Adam at the last minute. I bought Ash recently and he's supposed to be quiet and sensible, but I want to see what he's like for myself. It would be *gut* to see how he is with another horse," he added.

Diana did not want to go riding with Jethro if he was about to tell her he was engaged. Still, she could not tear herself away from him.

Diana saddled Snow and the two of them walked away from the stables at a leisurely pace. Diana wondered if Jethro would broach the subject first, or whether she would have to come straight out and ask him.

After a long silence, Diana could not stand it any longer. When they reached the trail through the woods, she asked, "Jethro, what did you want to talk to me about, yesterday?" She stole a glance at Jethro's face and he looked awkward. *Oh no, here we go!* she thought. *At least I will have abs of steel, with all this stomach-clenching.*

"Diana, I don't know quite how to tell you this."

Oh no, Diana thought, *here it comes*.

"You might be quite upset when I tell you this, but I hope we can remain friends."

Diana winced, and steeled herself for the worst.

Jethro continued. "I don't know how to tell you this, but Constantine Connors is not quite what he seems."

Diana was puzzled. "Constantine? Whatever do you mean?"

"I mean, I'm afraid to say, he is not an honest man." Jethro brought Ash to a stop and turned to look at Diana.

Diana halted Snow too. "Yes, I know. I happened to meet up with Abigail Briskey and she told me all about him."

It was Jethro's turn to be puzzled. "You know? And you're not upset?"

"Upset? Why would I be upset? Well, it was a horrible thing he did to Abigail, and I'm worried about Lori and Dad, but I'm not sure what you're getting at."

Jethro looked decidedly uncomfortable. "I mean, with you dating him and all."

"What?" Diana almost shrieked. "I am *not* dating Constantine Connors. Whatever gave you such an idea?"

The look on Jethro's face was a mixture of puzzlement, confusion, and relief.

"I saw the two of you having dinner the other night."

Diana shook her head. "Oh yes, how did I forget that?"

Jethro still looked puzzled, so she continued. "Aunt Evangeline asked me to have dinner with her, and led me to believe just the two of us would be having dinner. Behind my back, she also invited Constantine. It was her attempt to matchmake. An *unsuccessful* attempt," she added.

"So you and Constantine never dated? Lavender seemed to think you and Constantine were very close at the park."

"No, not at all. Constantine's been pursuing me against my wishes, and before that, he was pursuing Celeste too. After I spoke to Abigail, I figured that he might've thought we were

wealthy, and was after our money. Turns out
that there's a Trust Fund for us. Constantine,
being Dad's lawyer, would know that, although
thankfully Aunt Evangeline told us that the
trustee is from a different law firm."

Jethro did not respond. Diana did not want to
go through the whole matter of the Trust
again, so gathered courage and blurted out,
"Are you and Lavender engaged?"

"No." It was Jethro's turn to sound surprised.
"Whatever gave you that idea?"

Diana's heart was leaping happily. "Someone
suggested it, and I thought that's what you
wanted to tell me yesterday."

Jethro shook his head. "No, I wanted to speak
to you about Constantine Connors."

The two rode along the trail in silence. Diana
hoped Jethro would speak again, but he didn't
say a word, at least not on personal matters.

The two discussed the woods, the birds in the woods, and the weather.

Jethro looked across at her and smiled, one of those rare smiles where his eyes seemed to bore right into her. "So, you're not going to move back to New York? Have you found you've missed us too much to leave?"

"Oh, um, oh," was all Diana could manage. *Why does Jethro have this effect on me?* She smiled and ducked her head.

Diana arrived back at the stables in a state of near bliss. Things appeared to be going very well with Jethro, better than she had hoped for.

Diana had only just dismounted from Snow when a car drove up at too fast a speed for being around horses. Lavender leaped out of the car. "Jethro, I need to speak to you. Sorry, Diana, I didn't see you there." She looked sheepish.

"I'll take Snow to the wash bay," Diana said. They had only walked and Snow was not even sweating, but Lavender clearly wanted to speak with Jethro in private.

I wonder what that's about? Diana thought. *One step forward and two steps backward. Perhaps Jethro and Lavender are dating, after all. When Jethro said they weren't engaged, maybe he simply meant he hadn't asked her yet.*

After Diana washed Snow and scraped her down to remove excess moisture, she led her back to her stall, and then carried the saddle and bridle to the tack room. Jethro and Lavender were standing close, their heads together, and Lavender was talking. They both looked up when Diana entered. Diana noted that Lavender looked uneasy, if not a little embarrassed.

"Here, let me take those." Jethro took the saddle and bridle from Diana. As he removed the saddle from her arm, their fingers touched. Diana hoped Jethro did not notice her sharp intake of breath.

"Thanks, Jethro. Bye, see you later, Lavender."

"Diana, there's no need to rush off," Jethro said.

"I'd better get going, Jethro." With that, Diana left the stable and walked back to the Stone House, crestfallen. With every crunch of her feet on the gravel, Diana's mind seemed to change. Was Jethro interested in her, or not? Was Lavender interested in him? It seemed so. But if that were in fact the case, was Jethro interested in Lavender?

CHAPTER NINETEEN

Diana shook herself awake and then sat up. Celeste was standing over her and talking quickly. "The what? What did you say, Celeste?"

"The Amish fundraiser dinner!"

Diana yawned and stretched. "What time is it?"

"It's not today."

"No, what time is it now? I was having a nice dream."

"Never mind that. This is exciting." Celeste sat down hard on Diana's bed.

"Stop bouncing on my bed, Celeste! That could be fun. I've never been to an Amish fundraiser dinner before."

"You haven't?" Celeste looked surprised. "Well, you've been away for years. Allegra and I used to go to them, before, well, the financial disaster."

"What happens at that type of thing?"

"People buy stuff and maybe make donations."

Diana rolled her eyes. "I figured that. Do you know who else is going?"

"No."

Diana rubbed her eyes. "Celeste, start from the beginning and explain it all to me, slowly."

Celeste took a deep breath. "Okay, as I said, it's a fundraiser. The announcer will say something, and while he's doing that, people will eat. Then there'll be things to be auctioned. People write down their names and the prices they want to pay for something. You know, a silent auction."

"What sort of things?" Diana yawned again.

"I don't know. It's different every time, just whatever people have donated. It could be anything really, someone who owns an electronics store might have donated an electrical item, and a jeweler could donate cheaper items. Amish people might donate pies, the cheaper things."

"Why cheaper items?"

"Well, because the expensive things get auctioned in the main auction just before or after dessert."

"Dessert? I'm starving already."

Celeste ignored her. "People are encouraged to walk around the room and bid on items which are located just off to the side. Last time I went, there were around sixty items."

Diana was thrilled at the prospect of seeing Jethro again but was worried that Lavender might be there. "How's Dad today?"

"Much better, but Lori is in with him."

"Lori!" Diana gasped. "What, so early?"

Celeste nodded. "We're going to have to do something about that."

"I know, but what? Dad's so stubborn. We can't exactly be forthright and tell him that Lori's after his money... well, *our* money."

Celeste nodded again. "Actually, I've never really thought that out too clearly. He doesn't have any money, so I suppose she thinks when we come into our money, he'll have enough to share."

"True. Who will he listen to? We'll have to get some help with this. Dad won't listen to us."

"He'll listen to Constantine, unfortunately."

"Yes, exactly, more's the pity. Who else will he listen to?"

Both girls looked at each other and said in unison, "Aunt Evangeline!"

"The trouble is," Diana said, "Aunt Evangeline thinks Lori is a paragon of virtue and Constantine is a charming, eligible bachelor."

"What about if we spell it out to her? If we explain it all, maybe she will listen to us."

"I don't like our chances, Celeste, but it's worth a try. It's all I can think of. You call her while I go to the bathroom."

"What will I say?"

Diana hopped out of bed. "Say we both need to talk with her, and as soon as possible. Make sure you don't tell her what it's about. We need to speak with her in person. Offer to go over there, or say we can meet her out somewhere. It's best if we don't speak here and risk being overheard."

Aunt Evangeline was able to meet the girls that day, but wanted them to meet her at a shopping mall over an hour away.

The day was not a pleasant one for driving, being overcast. The rain was falling softly, but that only served to make the weather humid and disagreeable. The traffic was unusually heavy as well.

Celeste spotted Aunt Evangeline getting out of her metallic silver BMW sedan as they were looking for a parking place. Diana was waiting for a man to reverse so she could take his spot, when another car sped up, ducked behind the reversing car, and took the spot. Celeste and Diana groaned.

"Diana, quick, let me out here. I don't think Aunt Evangeline has seen us and she's heading over there. Meet us over there when you find a parking place."

Diana let Celeste out of the car, and then drove around and around until she found a parking place. The heat on the walk to the mall was oppressive.

Aunt Evangeline and Celeste were waiting for her. "Girls, do we need coffee before we start?" Aunt Evangeline asked.

Diana and Celeste nodded. The three of them went in search of a café, and finally found a little place that looked promising. After they ordered, Diana brought up the subject of Constantine.

"Aunt Evangeline, the other day we were telling you about Constantine Connors, and you basically said he was a fine, upstanding citizen, and so on."

Evangeline pursed her lips. "Yes, *I* think so."

"Aunt Evangeline, I met an old friend, Abigail Briskey, the other day. Constantine Connors was business partners with her husband and tricked him out of his money, and Abigail's husband went bankrupt."

Aunt Evangeline was not visibly perturbed by Diana's comments, and simply said, "There are two sides to every story, dear."

Diana sighed. "Aunt Evangeline, Jethro Wittmer also told me that Constantine Connors is not to be trusted. He knows what happened to Abigail and her husband, and Abigail said the Wittmers have had to help her out financially."

Diana expected Evangeline to dismiss her comments, but to her surprise, Aunt Evangeline took her seriously.

"Really? Are you sure? Did Jethro tell you this?"

"Yes, Aunt Evangeline. Abigail told me, and then Jethro told me. There can be no doubt."

Celeste intervened. "And what we are *really* worried about, is Lori and Dad."

Evangeline frowned deeply. "Lori really likes Ethan. She's been a good friend to him. Honestly, I don't know what he would have done without her. She's been such a support."

Diana was starting to get exasperated. "Aunt Evangeline, think about it! Lori is Constantine's sister. Let's get back to Constantine for a moment. How do you feel about him now? Are you willing to accept he's not what he seems?"

Aunt Evangeline pondered the matter. "I suppose I have to face the facts, but he seems such a nice man. It's hard to believe he's a con man." After seeing Diana's face, Evangeline added, "But I suppose that must be the case then, if what you say is true."

It was Celeste's turn. "And since you now know what Constantine is like, does Lori's relationship with Dad worry you at all?"

"Well dear, I don't know that they're tarred with the same brush. Let's talk about this later. How about we go looking for dresses? I need two or three."

Celeste and Diana both sighed, but could do nothing other than follow Aunt Evangeline as she strode away to the nearest clothing store.

Diana and Celeste were bored, as Aunt Evangeline took what seemed forever to choose dresses. She all but told the owner of the expensive little boutique her life history. The owner encouraged her to try on styles she would not have otherwise considered, and consequently Aunt Evangeline tried on several outfits.

She extolled the virtues of all of her purchases at some length. "Look girls, I have these adorable little dresses and these gorgeous sweaters. Aren't they totally flattering! They look like they were designed just for me. Look at this beautiful magenta leopard print, and this one, with its gorgeous fall colors. Don't they go well with the lime green stripes!"

Her speech roused the girls from their stupor. They had all but fallen asleep in the comfortable armchairs.

"Are you trying on any more clothes?" Diana asked warily.

"No, I'm happy with what I got. Unless you've spotted something else that you think would suit me?"

"No!" both girls said in unison.

"I'll pay, and then let's have lunch."

Aunt Evangeline said that lunch was her treat, and that they should drive to a restaurant she liked. Diana again had trouble finding a parking place. The unseasonal humidity had risen and was most uncomfortable, although Celeste and Aunt Evangeline did not seem to notice it.

The restaurant was crowded and noisy. Clumps of sinister, ominous thunderclouds gave the sky the appearance of an old English oil painting. The steel and barely-upholstered chairs looked minimalist and austere although were surprisingly comfortable, but the pink and brown patterned carpet looked faded, and even not too clean in places. Diana wondered why Evangeline had recommended the place.

After they ordered, Diana once more raised the subject of Lori and Ethan. "Aunt Evangeline, Celeste and I want you to help us. We have no one else to turn to," she pleaded. "We don't trust Constantine, and we're quite sure he's after our money, as he knows about the Trust Fund. As Lori is his sister and is a little *too* friendly with Dad for our liking, this makes us worried. That's reasonable, isn't it?"

Evangeline thought for a while before answering. "I suppose so. Hmm, I do understand why you're worried, but Lori seems such a lovely person."

Celeste piped up. "Aunt Evangeline, haven't you ever seen reporters interviewing neighbors after the police arrest a con man? All the neighbors say how surprised they are and that they thought the guy was a lovely, charming man."

"I suppose so." Aunt Evangeline did not appear convinced.

"You're a good matchmaker. Can't you think of someone else to match Dad up with?" Diana winked at Celeste.

Aunt Evangeline seemed to perk up. "Someone instead of Lori?"

Both Celeste and Diana nodded.

"I can't think of anyone offhand, but I'll certainly put my mind to it."

"Thanks, Aunt Evangeline," Diana said. "Do you think you can keep an eye on Lori and report any suspicions to Dad? I mean, how would you feel if she was only after him for our money? It's a very awkward situation, with Constantine being Dad's lawyer and

Constantine's sister, Lori, clearly wanting a relationship with Dad, and we know for a fact that Constantine is a con man."

Aunt Evangeline looked alarmed. "Yes, since you put it like that, it's a very awkward situation. A very awkward situation indeed."

CHAPTER TWENTY

Diana and Celeste had spent the morning rummaging through the spare room which had been turned into a storage room, when Ethan and Celeste had vacated the Main House.

"I didn't realize we had so much stuff," Celeste exclaimed after the two had sorted through the umpteenth carton. "We sold off a lot of furniture too."

"It doesn't help that they're not labeled." Diana sat down on the worn rug over the polished wood floor. "This is going to take forever."

"And the thing is, any important papers that Mom had would be at her lawyers' anyway."

Diana nodded, and then sighed. "Let's keep going until lunch time and then we can take a break."

Celeste cut through tape on the next carton and then exclaimed, "Diana, look what I've found!"

Diana took the beautifully embroidered doilies from the top of the carton. "These must have been Grannie's, or maybe even her mother's."

Celeste admired the delicate linen. "Look at all that embroidery and crochet work."

"That's actually tatting, and the cotton's so fine. That would have taken ages to do."

"What's tatting?" Celeste held the delicate

doily up to the light and ran her finger around the edge.

"It's kind of a knot and you can do lace edging with it. I used to be able to do it. Do you have some string? I can show you how to do it."

Celeste hurried out and returned with a length of string. Diana showed her how to do tatting, using just her finger. "And you do this with it so it doesn't slip." Diana looped the string around her finger.

"Wow, Diana, that's amazing." Celeste was clearly impressed. "That looks so complicated!"

Celeste lifted out the doilies and placed them carefully on top of another carton, then lifted Tiger out of the carton. Tiger had been trying to sharpen her claws on the top of a little wooden box at the bottom of the carton.

"You already have a scratching post, Tiger," Celeste said in exasperation. She lifted out the box and put it on the floor. When opened, it proved to be full of English paper pieced hexagons. "Diana, these were Mom's!"

"No, they were Grannie's, I'm sure."

The two girls exclaimed with delight as they pulled out and admired one one-inch hexagon after another.

"Diana, we should make these up," Celeste said, and then added, "Look at these old envelopes and postcards. I wonder why they're in the box?"

"They recycled them, back in those days."

"What do you mean, Diana? What did they use them for?"

"They used them to cut the hexagon shaped templates, to baste sew the fabric over, before they sewed them into blocks."

"Oh, wow." Celeste pulled out a postcard.

"Look, this one is dated from World War Two. How fascinating."

The girls both sat on the floor with the box between them. They carefully removed all the envelopes and sorted through them diligently.

"Celeste, look at this letter. It's dated 1895, and it's from a lawyer."

Celeste read through the letter. "The flowery handwriting is hard to understand, but it looks as if this guy was the family lawyer back then. What a shame it was so long ago."

Diana laughed. "I'll get my laptop and you make us both some coffee."

Diana returned and set up her laptop on top of a group of cartons, and then sat on what appeared to be a more substantial carton. "Celeste!"

"I'm coming!" Celeste walked back into the room with two steaming mugs.

"Thanks." Diana took a sip then gasped. "This is disgusting, seriously, Celeste."

"But you like your coffee strong."

"Yes, but not so strong that I could stand a spoon up in it."

Celeste laughed. "Sorry, I was in a hurry. I'll make you another one."

"No, don't bother, but could you just put some hot water in it, to thin it down a bit?"

Celeste disappeared with the cup, and then returned with something that looked less like molasses.

"Thanks, much better. Now, what was that name again?"

"Smythe-Rigby."

Celeste consulted the old, yellowing piece of paper and nodded.

"Was the address in Harrisburg Avenue, by any chance?"

"You're kidding. Is the law firm still there?"

"Yes. It's now called *Smythe-Rigby and Serna*."

"Diana, this means that the Trustee is most likely from this law firm."

"I hope so. We should call Aunt Evangeline."

Celeste called Aunt Evangeline and put the phone on loudspeaker, and held it between herself and Diana. For once, Aunt Evangeline answered promptly. "Hello, Celeste, I'm at golf."

"Sorry to disturb you, Aunt Evangeline."

"That's okay. I'm at the nineteenth hole."

"Do you want to call back when you've finished the game?"

Aunt Evangeline laughed. "Celeste, the nineteenth hole is what golfers say when they're having a cool drink after finishing the game."

"Oh. Well, Diana and I were going through some of Mom's old stuff, and we think we've found her law firm. Would you very much mind calling them for us please and asking? We don't know where to start."

"Of course, I will. Wait a moment until I find a pen and paper. Go ahead, what's the name?"

"Smythe-Rigby and Serna." Celeste dictated the number.

"Leave it with me. I'll call them when I get home."

Celeste and Diana went to the kitchen to make some lunch. Diana looked into the depths of the refrigerator and found some tomato pasta. "Celeste, what about tomato pasta?"

"Sounds good."

Just then, the doorbell rang. The girls looked at each other. "Lori?" Diana asked.

"You start the pasta, I'll get the door."

To Diana's surprise, Celeste returned with Jethro.

"What are you doing here?" Diana blurted out without thinking.

"I came to see Ethan. How is he?"

"Asleep," Celeste said. "He's doing much better, though. Would you like some lunch? Diana is a good cook."

"It's only reheated tomato pasta, I'm afraid," Diana said as she took the bowl out of the microwave.

"I'd love to stay for lunch, thank you, and no Diana, you won't dissuade me by belittling your baking. You won't get rid of me that easily."

"But, um, but," Diana stammered, tripping

over her words. *Oh dear, Jethro thought I was trying to get rid of him. I wasn't, not at all.*

The three of them were soon sitting around the table enjoying the meal that Diana had quickly rustled up. Diana considered that this was how life would have been, had she not broken off her engagement with Jethro. She had missed the happy family gatherings, and had not even kept in touch with her own family, as she should have. *That changes from this minute forward*, Diana told herself.

Jethro stood as soon as he'd eaten, much to Diana's disappointment.

She showed Jethro to the door. As she opened it, he turned to her and was about to say something, but Aunt Evangeline was standing on the doorstep.

"Oh you gave me quite a fright," she exclaimed. "I lifted up my hand to ring the doorbell, and I hadn't even touched it when the door opened. I thought it was one of those new-fangled technology things."

Jethro and Evangeline laughed, but Diana was frustrated. *Why does everybody show up when I'm about to have a private conversation with Jethro?* she wondered as Jethro left.

Aunt Evangeline showed herself in. "Diana, I have some news and I wanted to tell you both in person. Where's Celeste?"

Celeste by this time had come out of the kitchen to see what was taking Diana so long.

"Now girls, I've spoken to the law firm and it turns out that they've been your mother's family's law firm for a very long time. Of course, they wouldn't tell me anything, but they did ask you to call a Mr. Serna." She pulled out a piece of paper with Mr. Serna's details and handed it to Diana. "Since you're both concerned about Lori and Constantine, he might be able to give you some help. As Constantine is Ethan's lawyer, Mr. Serna should be able to advise you on that matter as well."

"Come in," Celeste said. "We're looking through the old family stuff."

The three of them spent a wonderful afternoon looking through the box of postcards, envelopes and paper pieced hexagons.

As Aunt Evangeline was about to leave, her parting words were, "I almost forgot. Have you heard the news? It seems Lavender is going to convert to Amish."

CHAPTER TWENTY-ONE

After Evangeline left, Celeste turned to Diana. "Are you all right, Diana? You've gone as white as a sheet."

Diana realized her hands were trembling. "I'm shocked that Lavender is thinking about becoming Amish."

"Lavender's grandmother was born Amish and only left on her *rumspringa*," Celeste reminded her. "Her grandmother eventually went back to the Amish and has stayed there ever since.

You know that. Why is it a surprise that Lavender is joining the community?"

Diana shook her head. "Celeste, hardly anybody ever joins the Amish community. I can't see that having a grandmother who was once Amish but left and then went back to the Amish would make Lavender any more likely to join the Amish than any other *Englischer*."

Celeste disagreed. "We grew up with the Wittmers. They lived next door. We're used to the Amish ways and Lavender is even more so, and you nearly became Amish. Plus, she's always been a quiet girl and not interested in fashion or the latest movies or anything like we are. Why are you so upset about Lavender?"

Diana was thinking about how to respond when Celeste let out a squeal. She planted her palm on her forehead. "Diana!" she shrieked. "You're still in love with Jethro!"

Diana looked around her. "Hush, Celeste." She took her by the arm to the porch and shut the front door firmly behind them. "I don't want anyone to overhear."

"Dad is asleep and the nurse won't care. It's not as if Lori is listening."

"Lori's here?"

"No, I just said that. Diana, you look like you're about to cry. Just how bad is it?"

Diana put her face in her hands. "Celeste, what have I done? I shouldn't have left. I shouldn't have broken off the engagement. I was spoiled, and young and silly. I've regretted it ever since."

Celeste reached over and patted her shoulder. "If you regretted it, why didn't you come straight back home?"

"Because I thought it was the right thing to do. I thought I could never become Amish."

Celeste tapped her chin. "And when did you realize you *could* become Amish?"

"Not for years. Maybe I had to get older in order to come to my senses. I 've always been in love with Jethro, though."

Celeste wagged her finger at her. "Obviously, you didn't love him *enough*."

Diana was shocked. "What do you mean?"

"You didn't love him enough to become Amish for him."

Diana shook her head. "Don't you see? That was just it. I couldn't become Amish *just* for Jethro. It's a huge commitment and it wouldn't have been a good relationship if I wasn't able to adjust to the Amish way of life."

Celeste shot her a shrewd look. "And now?"

"I'd marry him in a heartbeat and become Amish now," Diana admitted, "if he'd have me. But it looks as though he's marrying

Lavender." She did her best not to burst into sobs.

"Come on, let's go for a walk," Celeste said. "You'll feel better than just sitting here going over and over your sorrows." When the two were walking through the grounds, Celeste added, "We don't know that there's anything between Jethro and Lavender."

"But you said so yourself."

"Those were empty words, Diana. I just assumed that without giving the matter any thought. If you're still in love with Jethro, then he might well still be in love with you."

Diana laughed ruefully. "It doesn't work like that."

Celeste took Diana by the shoulders and turned her to face her. "How do you know? Why did he want you to help with his children? And why did his mother leave them with you instead of with

Lavender or any number of Amish women?"

Diana shrugged and the two walked on. Diana stopped to pick a Townsend daisy and twirled it between her fingers. "You heard what Naomi said. She wants Rose and Sarah to become more used to *Englischers*. That would make sense if Lavender was going to marry Jethro."

"It would make more sense if Jethro was still in love with you," Celeste pointed out.

Diana put her hand to her head. "This is giving me a headache."

"You'll have to ask Jethro."

Diana stopped walking. "Celeste, are you mad? I can't ask Jethro!"

"Why not? Then you'd know the answer."

"Yes, and what if he says he's in love with Lavender? Then I'd be horribly embarrassed.

Besides, I thought he wanted to tell me something and I figure he wants to tell me he's going to ask Lavender to marry him."

"He might want to tell you that he's bought a new buggy or a new horse or something."

Diana sighed long and hard. "Seriously, Celeste, I'm fairly certain he's going to tell me he's marrying Lavender. I think that's why he wanted me to help with the children. He wants to ease them into our culture. That makes sense."

"It does make sense," Celeste admitted, "but it would make just as much sense if he was going to marry you."

Diana sat down hard on the grass. "This is such a mess. I wish I'd never come home."

Celeste sat next to Diana on the grass. "You don't mean that! And you had to come home because of Dad."

"Sure, but I should've gone back to New York.

As it is, I've resigned and given up my apartment, and now that I'm here, I'll see Jethro and Lavender together every day."

"You don't know that for certain," Celeste said. "You're jumping to conclusions. You're building it all up in your mind when you don't know any of the facts. And anyway, Diana, do you truly think you could become Amish?"

Diana nodded slowly. "I've given it a lot of thought. You know how the Amish young people go on *rumspringa* to sample our ways and get it out of their system, and then they decide whether they're going to commit to the community or not?" Celeste nodded. Diana pushed on. "That's how I feel. It's like my ten years in New York were some sort of long *rumspringa*."

"A *very* long *rumspringa*," Celeste said with a chuckle. "So, you think you've gotten it all out of your system and now you can be Amish?"

Diana nodded slowly. "Yes, now that I've come

home, I can see how much I missed the slower pace of life. I've enjoyed the baking and the knitting I've done with Rose and Sarah. I've enjoyed the sense of community."

Diana expected Celeste to protest in some way, so she was surprised when she didn't. "I know what you mean. I've often thought I'd be happy to be Amish."

Diana was shocked by her words. "You would?"

"Yes, I enjoyed all the time we spent with the Amish when we were growing up. They have happy families and I love the sense of community. It's safe there. You know that if something happens to you that someone's always got your back. I guess I kind of crave that safety and security."

"You know you've mentioned it before," Diana said, frowning. "Is it because of Jeremiah?"

Celeste flushed red and made an unladylike,
snorting sound. "Jeremiah! Of course not. He's
been my best friend since we were children. I
could never marry Jeremiah," she added with a
laugh.

Diana thought she had better change the
subject as Celeste's face was growing redder
and redder by the minute. "You know, I think
I will go and speak with the bishop."

"What will you say to him exactly?" Celeste
asked her. "Will you tell him how you feel
about Jethro?"

Diana bit her lip. "I don't know. I think I
would be too embarrassed to say that. The
thing is, I've been worried that the whole
community resents me for leaving Jethro like I
did when I was supposed to become Amish
and marry him. Maybe, the bishop is still mad
with me too. I'd like to get that straightened
out."

Celeste chuckled. "Oh Diana, you know, the

Amish never resent anyone. They forgive *everybody*. Seriously, I don't know what you're worried about. Still, I think it would clear your head if you spoke with the bishop."

"But what if he refuses to speak with me?"

Celeste continued to laugh. "Diana, for someone who would be happy to join the Amish, you certainly don't seem to know much about them. Of course, the bishop will speak with you. Hopefully, he might even drop hints about what's happening with Lavender and then you'll know where you stand."

"I hope so," Diana said in a small voice.

"Honestly, Diana, I think you're worried about nothing. I really don't think Jethro likes Lavender. I doubt he's going to marry Lavender. Maybe, Lavender has her eye on some other Amish man. Or maybe she's just drawn to that way of life considering how close she is with her Amish grandmother."

A small glimmer of hope arose within Diana. "Maybe you're right."

Celeste nodded. "You know, the more I think about it, the more I think I *am* right. I doubt Jethro would ask you to help with his children if he didn't still feel the same way about you. Besides, he didn't remarry after his wife passed away. Maybe, he was still pining after you. All the single Amish ladies in the community wanted to marry him."

Diana narrowed her eyes, unprepared for the pang of jealousy that shot through her at Celeste's words. "How do you know that?"

"I'm good friends with Jeremiah, of course," Celeste said, rolling her eyes. "Everyone was talking about it."

"Why didn't you ever tell me any of this? About Jethro, I mean. You didn't even tell me he was married."

Celeste was clearly exasperated. She held up

both hands, palms upward, to the sky. "Diana, you told me not to. You made it very clear. You said I wasn't to tell you a single thing about Jethro, no matter what. You said I was never to mention his name to you again."

Diana bit her lip and stared at a patch of white flowers. How had her life turned out the way it had? But was Celeste right? Was talk of Lavender joining the Amish community nothing to do with Jethro?

And would she get a second chance at love?

CHAPTER TWENTY-TWO

Diana drove straight to the bishop's house before she had a chance to change her mind. She had no idea what she wanted to say to him, but she knew it would put her mind at ease. When she stopped her car outside the bishop's house, it occurred to her that he might not even be home. Tentatively, she walked up the stairs and across the front porch and knocked on the door.

A short, plump woman opened the door.

Diana recognized her as the bishop's wife, Anna.

She stared at Diana and then shot her a wide smile. "Diana! *Wilkom*. You want to speak with my husband?"

Diana nodded. "Yes, I'd like to. Is he at home?"

"*Nee*, but I expect him home at any minute. Please come inside and share some meadow tea with me."

The kindly woman showed Diana inside and indicated she should sit on a chair. "It's a lovely day, isn't it?" Anna said with a smile. With that, she disappeared, leaving Diana alone with her thoughts for a few moments.

Her stomach churned and her palms became sweaty. She began to wish she hadn't come, after all. What on earth would she say to the bishop? And would he lecture her?

Anna returned with a large mug of steaming liquid and placed it on a little wooden table beside Diana. The smell of mint was overpowering, and although Diana usually liked meadow tea, the scent made her feel a little nauseous. "Please help yourself to some peach pie," Anna said. "When my husband comes, he'll finish it all." She broke off with a laugh.

Diana simply smiled and nodded.

"So, we haven't seen you around these parts in... Well, how long has it been?"

"Ten years," Diana said.

Anna's eyes shot skyward. "Ten years? It seems like only yesterday that you left. Where are you living now?"

"I've been living in New York, but I've recently moved home."

Anna nodded slowly. "And how is your father?"

"His health is much better now, *denki*," Anna said. Silently, she added, *A pity the same couldn't be said for his temper.* She smiled wryly.

"I heard you took Jethro Wittmer's *dochders*, Rose and Anna, to the knitting circle," Anna continued.

Anna felt her cheeks burn. Was that a pointed comment, or was Anna merely making conversation? It seems the bishop's wife knew everything that happened in these parts. She ducked her head and simply said, "*Jah*."

"They're delightful children, are they not?" Without waiting for Diana to respond, Anna pushed on. "It's been difficult for them without a *mudder*. Of course, Naomi does as much as she can, but with all those *menner* in the house..." Her words trailed away and she gave a shrug.

"Yes, it must be hard for her with all her sons at home as well as her two grandchildren."

Anna readily agreed. "And Naomi looks after the children when Jethro is at work all day with his brothers in the business. It will be *gut* when Jethro marries again. It will heal his heart, and also his *fraa* will be a wonderful help for Naomi."

Diana set sat bolt upright. "Jethro is getting married again?"

Anna looked shocked. "Oh, I didn't exactly say that. I just meant if he did. You know, one day." She shifted in her seat uncomfortably and looked down at her meadow tea.

The bishop's wife does know something she's not telling me, Diana thought. Her heart was beating out of her chest. At that moment, Bishop Eberly appeared at the door.

He smiled widely when he saw Diana. "Diana! *Wunderbar*! I was hoping we could chat sometime. Is that peach pie?"

Diana immediately felt at ease. She remembered the bishop as being kindly, but she didn't know how he would react to her after what she had done.

"I'll fetch you some meadow tea," Anna said to her husband.

The bishop helped himself to a piece of peach pie. "Are you eating some more?" he asked Diana, indicating her empty plate.

She shook her head.

Anna promptly returned with a cup of meadow tea and set it beside her husband. "Well, I'll leave you to chat," she said with a smile and left the room.

"Well, I expect you're wondering why I'm here," Diana said.

"I wanted to speak with you. Nau is awwer bsll Zert!" *Now it's about time!*

Diana nodded slowly. "I want to apologize for what I did ten years ago, breaking off my engagement and fleeing to New York without a word to anybody, apart from Jethro, that is."

"And have you apologized to Jethro?"

Diana was shocked. "No! How silly of me. Why didn't that occur to me? I feel terrible."

The bishop smiled at her. "We can't worry about the past. We can never change anything in the past, but we can change the future. You have plenty of time to apologize to Jethro, if it is in your heart to do so."

Diana nodded vigorously. "Yes, yes, of course I want to apologize to him." She shook her head slowly. "I don't know why it didn't occur to me."

"Sometimes we don't see the things that are most obvious to us," the bishop said.

I wonder what he meant by that? Diana thought.

The bishop didn't say anything, and Diana was uncomfortable with the silence. It prompted her to speak, although she tripped over her words. "I was in love with Jethro when I went to New York, but I didn't feel I could live in the community as an Amish person. I wanted to see more of the world."

"And now you have seen more of the world." The bishop said it as a statement not a question.

Diana nodded. "Yes, and I'm much older now. I was young and foolish then. I feel like a bad Christian, but I didn't pray and trust in God over the situation."

The bishop leaned forward in his chair. "Being a Christian doesn't make somebody perfect. Everybody is flawed. Christians make bad decisions and have bad days just like anybody else. It's just that Christians have *Gott* who is ready to help them. All we have to do is turn to Him and ask."

"I didn't ask," Diana said in a small voice. "I just, I just ran away."

"But all that is in the past," the bishop said. "Now, you can press onto the future and leave the past behind you."

"Yes, that sounds simple and makes perfect sense when you say it like that," Diana said. She wanted to ask more, but she was too embarrassed.

However, it seemed the bishop knew she had something else on her mind. "Is there anything you'd like to talk about?" he asked.

Diana bit her lip before answering. "Um, I'm not really sure. I ran away from the Amish before, so if I do want to join the community again, what would happen?"

"You were never baptized into the community," the bishop said, "and you did not receive the instruction. If you wish to be baptized into the community, you would need to take the instruction over eighteen weeks."

"So, I wouldn't be punished because I wanted to become Amish once before, but I ran away? There wouldn't be any black marks against me?"

The bishop chuckled. "*Nee*, and I know it wouldn't be a decision that you would take lightly. You've had ten years to think about this. As I told you ten years ago, not many *Englischers* have joined the communities. It's rare. Ours is an entirely different way of life, as you realize. Still, our community is one which is open to seekers. Many communities are not."

Diana nodded slowly.

"And you would have to be entirely sure of what is in your heart," the bishop continued. "Are you?"

Does he mean Jethro? Diana wondered. She dared not ask him. Instead, she nodded. "*Jah.*"

She would have said more, but there was a knock on the door. Anna walked into the room, smiled at Diana, and then crossed to open the front door. Diana was shocked to see Lavender there.

"Oh, I'm sorry, I didn't know you had company," Lavender said, clearly concerned to see Diana.

Diana stood up. "I'm sorry. I called by to visit with the bishop without warning."

Lavender waved her back down. "I can come back at a later time."

"No, that's fine," Diana said. "I was just leaving." She turned to the bishop. "Thank you so much."

"Come back and talk any time," he said.

Diana thanked him again and hurried out the

door. So then, Lavender *was* going to join the Amish community. There was no other reason she would visit the bishop.

Still, maybe Celeste was right and Lavender simply wanted to join the community for reasons other than to do with Jethro.

Diana clung to that hope as she drove home.

CHAPTER TWENTY-THREE

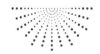

Diana was glad she had taken extra care with her make-up and clothes that morning.

At first she had thought allowing Celeste to do her make-up was a mistake, but it turned out she had a skillful touch with make-up. Diana wanted the natural look, and Celeste had assured her that the natural look would take a lot of work. Diana was thankful Celeste hadn't asked her why she wanted the natural look or suggested that it was for the benefit of Jethro.

Diana did, however, refuse to wear the high heels. These were no mere heels; they were taller than any heels Diana had worn before, and besides, she was used to trainers. The easiest way to get around New York was on foot.

Diana stood in front of the mirror, applying more lip gloss and mentally trying to psych herself up for seeing Jethro. No doubt, she would see him soon. She and Celeste had arrived at the fundraiser early.

When Diana went back to the table, she was surprised to see Abigail. They warmly embraced.

"You look wonderful, Abigail! Are you at our table?"

"Thanks, Diana. You look wonderful too. Yes, the Wittmers invited me. The proceeds of the fundraiser are going to the charity I used to work for."

Diana signaled to Celeste, who was standing close by. "Abigail, you remember Celeste, my sister?" The two shook hands. "Who else is at our table, do you know?"

"All four Wittmer brothers, Jethro, Ezra, Adam and Jeremiah, and Jessica and Lavender. Is Allegra coming?" Abigail asked.

Diana shook her head. "No, she and Larry flew to New York on business."

Abigail replied, but Diana did not hear what she said, as she looked up and saw Jethro walking toward her. It seemed as if she had stopped breathing. His copper hair poking out from under his hat reflected gold lights, and his shirt displayed to advantage his broad shoulders and the well-defined, bulging muscles in his arms. His strong jaw softened when he saw Diana.

He walked straight to her and stopped, still taller than she even in her heels. "Diana, you look beautiful."

Diana was glad the lights were dim as she was sure her face had flushed bright red. Diana simply looked up at Jethro, and did not speak. Who knows how long the two would have stood there, had they not been broken apart by Jeremiah needing Jethro's help.

"I told you, Diana!" Celeste whispered.

Diana looked around to see if anyone had heard. "Shush, Celeste!"

Abigail raised an eyebrow in amusement.

Oh no, what must she think? Diana wondered.

The guests were arriving, and Diana, Celeste, and Abigail were shown to their table. Lavender and Jessica were already seated, as were Adam and Ezra. Greetings were exchanged all around.

"How's your ankle, Lavender?"

"Good thanks, Celeste."

Diana noticed that Lavender seemed tense,

but chided herself for being paranoid. *Surely, there's nothing between Jethro and Lavender. If they were dating, Jethro wouldn't have shown any interest in me. But is Jethro interested in me, or does he only think of me as a good friend?* Diana's head was starting to spin. *Today should give me some answers on that score,* she thought.

Diana was distracted by the arrival of waiters serving appetizers, while a gentleman who was announced as the head of the charity started showing slides of what the charity was doing and explaining what the charity was all about. Diana found it hard to hear, as the crowd was murmuring softly and the waiters were none too quiet. Jethro and Jeremiah were still absent.

After the entrée, people were encouraged to walk around the room and bid on the silent auction. Diana didn't see anything that took her fancy.

"Diana!" Celeste ran up to her excitedly.

"Jeremiah just told me that the last block of the Album Quilt has just been signed! That means forty-two people have now made a large donation."

"That's wonderful, Celeste, and by the time it's auctioned, you'll have raised a large amount for charity."

Celeste could barely contain her excitement.

There was no sign of Jethro until the end of the main course, when he and Jeremiah appeared, ate some of their dinner hurriedly, and then made their apologies and left. Diana was sorely disappointed. She had been sure that she would have had some time with Jethro, yet the fundraiser was half over and she had hardly seen him at all.

Dessert arrived, which caused some good-natured bantering and swapping. Espresso foam over tiramisu and pistachio ice cream alternated with lemon soufflés in a white chocolate ramekin. No one seemed to want the dessert they were given, and wanted the dessert of the person next to them. Only Lavender did not join the good-humored disputes, and looked grim and downcast.

To Diana's delight, Jethro came back to the table. He took up his seat between Jessica and Lavender, and winked at Diana across the table.

Unfortunately for Diana, the table was too wide for conversation, and to her dismay, Lavender soon engaged Jethro in private conversation. Their voices were lowered and their heads were bent close to each other. The event was not turning out quite as Diana had hoped.

The main auction was riveting, and the amounts raised for charity were astounding. A diamond bracelet brought a huge sum, as did a holiday for six for ten days in Hawaii.

Finally, the time came for the auction of Celeste's Album Quilt. "Diana, here it is!"

"Ouch!" Diana winced as Celeste squeezed her arm.

The auctioneer expounded the history of Album Quilts. He told the audience that the Album Quilt was hand sewn and is an example of the Baltimore Album Quilt most popular from the 1840s to the 1890s. He explained that forty-two people had donated a certain amount, and so were able to sign their names in indelible ink on each of the forty-two blocks, and that the practice of signing names on quilts with indelible ink went back as far as 1840.

There were several bidders on the quilt, and although the bidding slowed down at the end, the quilt made a considerable sum, much to Celeste and Diana's delight.

Diana, however, was not listening to the exchange as Jethro was walking over in front of the stage. Even from this distance, he looked distracted, Diana thought, but then again he would have been busy as he was involved with the event. Diana noticed that Lavender kept looking behind her, no doubt wondering where Jethro was.

"Do you need some help to your feet?" Celeste asked Diana with a laugh. "You did eat a lot."

Diana laughed too.

"Abigail!"

The three girls turned around to see a young Amish lady. She was beautiful, with big blue eyes, and pale blonde hair showing around her bonnet.

"Josephine!" Abigail said. "I haven't seen you in ages. These are my friends, Diana and Celeste. Diana is an old friend and Celeste is her sister. Diana and Celeste, this is Josephine Beilier. Josephine lives in another Amish community but used to live in our old community." She turned back to Josephine. "Are you here for long?"

"*Nee.* It's *gut* to see you again, Abigail. I'm so sorry to hear of your news."

Abigail looked sad and murmured her thanks.

To change the subject, Diana said, "So, you're from another community? Did it take you long to get here?"

"I'm visiting to catch up with family and a friend or two, and then I have to go straight back home."

"That's very rushed," Celeste said. "What a change of pace for you."

As they were speaking, Diana was looking around for Jethro, but he was nowhere to be seen.

Jeremiah emerged from the shadowy depths from the direction of backstage and appeared startled to see Josephine. "Josephine, what a surprise! I mean, what a lovely surprise. We didn't know you would be here. Does"—he hesitated—"anybody else know you were coming?"

Diana was surprised to see Josephine blush.

"*Nee*, it was a spur of the moment decision. I only told my parents. I'm going back the day after tomorrow."

"Hmm." Jeremiah looked thoughtful and then turned to Celeste. "Celeste, the lady who bought the Album Quilt would like to meet you. She's thrilled about the quilt."

"I'd love to meet her. Come on, Diana, you helped me with it."

"I only did a tiny little bit, Celeste."

Celeste waved her hand in dismissal. "Nonsense, you were a great help. Come with me, anyway." Celeste linked her arm through Diana's and followed Jeremiah. As they neared a section to the left of the stage, they heard someone calling Jeremiah's name.

"Just through there," Jeremiah said. "I have to go and help out here, then I'll be right back, but go ahead and introduce yourself."

The lighting was good in this section, and Diana looked at the beaming lady ahead. However, it was the little section off to the left that caught her eye. Lavender was standing close to Jethro. They were both whispering to each other. To Diana, it appeared to be an intimate scene. Jethro looked up and saw Diana watching them. His face registered surprise.

Diana ran out of the room, ignoring Celeste calling after her. She ran toward the front doors. As she ran, her heel caught and she tripped heavily, snapping a strap and breaking her shoe. Embarrassed, she picked herself up and, without waiting to retrieve the shoe, hobbled outside.

Diana hurried to the nearest bathroom. Thankfully, she was alone in there, for she sobbed and sobbed until she thought her heart would break, and blew her nose noisily. She removed the other shoe, as it was hard to walk with one shoe.

Diana caught a taxi and cried all the way back to the Stone House. She repeatedly blew her nose loudly, and then at one point laughed aloud as she did feel like Cinderella after all, running from the ball and leaving a shoe behind. *Only Prince Charming won't be coming after me—he's in love with someone else*, she told herself. This made her cry even harder.

She noticed the taxi driver kept glancing back at her, but she didn't care. How could she have been so stupid? It had been ten years, after all. Why would she think Jethro still had feelings for her? He only thought of her as a friend. She had made such a fool of herself.

By the time Diana got back to the Stone House, she was a mess. Her eyes were swollen and puffy, and she had to catch her breath from sobbing for so long. Everything was crowding in on her. She hurried to her bedroom and hurriedly put on sweats and a tee. Her eyes fell on the piece of paper with the details of the lawyer provided by Aunt Evangeline, and Diana formed the beginnings of a plan. Maybe she could keep her apartment after all, and maybe Collette would let her have her old job back. She hurried to her laptop in the living room.

The sound of voices stirred her. They were coming from Ethan's room. Diana hurried to Ethan's room, only to find Lori sitting on the end of the bed. Tiger was sitting on the bed too, hissing at Lori at intervals, and occasionally swatting at her from a distance. Lori turned to look at Diana and her face was wearing a smug expression.

Diana ignored her. "Dad, are you all right?"

"Lori's visiting. I'm a bit tired."

Lori disregarded the hint. "We've just been watching a movie, Diana."

"Dad, I have to go back to New York now, but I'll be back soon, and I promise to visit frequently from now on." Diana gave Ethan a hug and a kiss, then sat on the other side of the bed and squeezed Ethan's hand.

"When do you leave?"

"I'm going to pack and then leave immediately. Something's come up." Diana could barely speak from choking back the tears.

"Call me as soon as you get there, Diana, no matter what the time?"

"I promise, Dad." Diana stood up, and bent down to kiss Ethan's cheek.

"And promise you'll be back soon?"

"I promise."

Ethan seemed to be drifting off to sleep, but

Lori made no move to leave. "Lori, Dad's asleep. I'll show you out."

Lori's face looked like a thundercloud. Diana was sure Lori would object, but she followed Diana to the door. "You can go out, too, Tiger." Diana picked up Tiger who was purring, and tried to hug her goodbye, but Tiger struggled.

As soon as Lori left, Diana threw her belongings together, and then composed a long note to Celeste. She was going back to New York.

CHAPTER TWENTY-FOUR

Diana couldn't bring herself to drive to New York, not just yet. She walked to the pond near the family home. It was where she always went to think, the peace of nature washing over her and steadying her heart. But right now, it was not working. She thought of Jethro, how he was set to marry Lavender. There was no other reason for Lavender to join the Amish than Jethro, and that made Diana's stomach churn. Thunder boomed overhead, and Diana knew how the sky felt, because her own heart was thundering too.

She plopped herself on the grass, and she watched the ducks in their steady sweep across the placid surface of the lake. Oh, how peaceful it would be to live life as a duck. Boring, too. But Diana craved boring, the type of boring which was filled with love and family and God. That was not boring to her, but to the world at large, the world which celebrated throwing your money away on clothes that would go out of fashion in two months and make-up that was filled with maybe dangerous and potentially harmful chemicals, floating across a pond would be boring.

"Diana."

Diana felt her heart stop. She knew that voice. She had dreamed of that voice for ten years. "Jethro?"

Diana was in shock; her mind had no way of processing Jethro's presence. She had so many questions, but did not know where to start.

Was he here to tell her he was marrying Lavender? That must be it. Diana didn't know if she wanted to have this conversation, but she asked God to fill her heart with grace.

"Diana, please hear me out. I have to explain about Lavender. I've asked her if I can, and she agreed. She feels really bad."

Diana shook her head, and the tears threatened to fall. "It's okay, Jethro. I'm so happy for you. I want you to be happy."

"Please hear me out, Diana. Lavender is in love with Ezra."

"Ezra?" Diana's mouth dropped open. She stood, but then she sat on the grass again. Jethro stepped shyly toward her and sat beside her by the edge of the pond.

"You met Jospehine Beilier last night?" he asked.

It was Diana's turn to nod.

"Please don't mention this matter to anyone apart from your sisters, but Ezra has been engaged to Josephine since they were teenagers. They've barely seen each other for years as her parents moved to another community. Lavender and Ezra have fallen in love, but Ezra has given his word to Josephine and won't break it."

Diana pressed a hand to her clammy forehead. Was she about to faint? She was absolutely about to faint. The shock of Jethro's announcement—even though it was not the announcement she had anticipated—made her feel sick.

"Ezra has tried to speak with Josephine," Jethro continued, "but she always comes up with a reason not to speak to him about their engagement. In fact, she avoids him. He'd like to break off the engagement—I can't even call it a relationship—but, of course, he needs to have a talk with Josephine to do so. And

346

obviously, he can't even begin a relationship with Lavender until his engagement with Josephine has been broken."

Things were starting to make sense. "Is that why Lavender was so upset," Diana replied, "because Josephine Beilier showed up at the fundraiser and no one knew she was back from her community?"

"*Jah*, and you thought you had seen us together."

Diana looked down, shamefaced.

"Didn't you notice we weren't alone? Jessica was standing next to Lavender."

Diana shook her head. "No. Oh, yes, I vaguely remember someone else there, but I was too upset."

"Why were you so upset?"

What a question, Diana thought, *he's put me on*

the spot. She ducked her head before looking back up at Jethro. He was smiling at her.

"How about we go for a walk? I think it's about to rain any minute."

Diana had a sudden thought. "How silly of me! I never even asked you—how did you know where to find me?"

"I know you like to think by the pond."

Diana blushed, but simply said, "Oh."

Diana and Jethro stood now. They began their steady walk around the pond, the breeze tugging Jethro's hair, and Diana jumping when another crack of thunder ripped the horizon apart.

"Diana, why did you break off our engagement ten years ago?" he said quietly.

Diana sighed. "Oh Jethro, I'm so dreadfully sorry. Will you ever forgive me? I've regretted that so many times since. I thought you must hate me."

"You fell out of love with me?"

"Oh no, Jethro, not at all. I'm so sorry. I was young and silly, and Aunt... um, I mean, I chose to listen to the wrong advice. I was afraid I'd lose myself being Amish. I just wanted to run away."

"Like you've run away now." Jethro said it as a statement of fact, not a question.

"No, I only came down to the pond."

It was raining now, but neither Diana nor Jethro seemed to notice. They were too focused on each other.

"Perhaps, but you were going back to New York. Celeste told me. She found your note."

"True, but it was all too much. I didn't know how you felt, and I kept thinking I had a chance with you, but then Lavender kept popping up. It was all too much."

"Diana, tell me, did you ever think about me when you were in New York?"

Diana took a deep breath. "Jethro, I thought of nothing else. You were always on my mind. I always thought about you, but I didn't know what to do about it. I thought you would be angry with me. I didn't know how to make it right."

"So, you had second thoughts about breaking the engagement?"

"Yes, almost immediately. I never fell out of love with you."

"Never?"

Diana shook her head, and then looked into Jethro's eyes. She was amazed at the passion and love she saw there. She longed for him. Diana felt her heart would burst with joy, as the ten years of love which had been tightly bottled were now given free rein.

The rain was light, but it was growing heavier by the second. "Jethro, we had better leave."

Jethro took her by the arm and pulled her close. "No, this can't wait. It's been delayed long enough."

To Diana's shock, Jethro got down on one knee on the wet grass.

That's not an Amish thing to do, Diana thought absently, scarcely believing her eyes.

The falling rain plastered his hair to his head. "Diana Hunt, I am madly in love with you, and have been since the first day I met you. I never stopped loving you. Would you do me the great honor of being my wife?"

Diana sobbed and flung her arms around Jethro's neck. He stood up and they kissed while clinging to each other in the rain. If either of them were

RUTH HARTZLER

thinking straight, they would have released each other from this embrace and darted for cover, but neither one was thinking straight. They were thinking of each other, of the ten years they had spent apart, of the life and the children they would have together now—now that God's plan had brought them here, to a small pond in a small community filled with big, beating hearts.

NEXT BOOK IN THIS SERIES

Match Made in Heaven

Will Celeste find love, or she is destined to remain single forever?

Celeste Hunt fancies herself as a matchmaker. Her handsome friend, the Amish mann Jeremiah Wittmer, warns her not to meddle with love, but his warnings fall on deaf ears. Her latest attempt to play Cupid for her new Amish friend has gone amiss in more ways than one.

NEXT BOOK IN THIS SERIES

Will Celeste's gift of matchmaking ruin her one true chance at happiness?

ABOUT RUTH HARTZLER

USA Today best-selling author, Ruth Hartzler, was a college professor of Biblical history and ancient languages. Now she writes faith-based romances, cozy mysteries, and archeological adventure.

Ruth Hartzler is best known for her Amish romances, which were inspired by her Brethren upbringing. When Ruth is not writing, she spends her time walking her dog and baking cakes for her adult children, all of whom have food allergies. Ruth also enjoys correcting grammar on shop signs when nobody is looking.

www.ruthhartzler.com

Made in United States
North Haven, CT
10 May 2024

52343273R00221